M000006325

"*The Twin* is a compelling and provocative narrative that will likely lead readers to a new understanding and appreciation of the overlap of spiritual and religious traditions."

—Kathleen Williams Renk, author
of *Vindicated: A Novel of Mary Shelley*

"*The Twin* is…a brilliant saga of the events, teachings, miracles, and personal life of Jesus, known as Yeshua. Complete with footnotes and translator notes, B.L. Treah, PhD, Professor of Classics, presents this easily readable fictional account in such an honest and straightforward way that one forgets it is not a true rendition of Jesus of Nazareth. Or maybe it is. History is merely an interpretation of events from the past, often tainted by perspective, and *The Twin* provides a new viewpoint that is highly entertaining and boldly unique. This is a novel that will wake you in the middle of the night tickling your senses as you grapple with the origins, life, and times of Jesus."

—Matthew Langdon Cost, author
of *Love in a Time of Hate*

"St. Jarre's knowledge of myth and religion is on full display in *The Twin*… St. Jarre invites us to ask questions, to look beneath story, and to 'not miss the point for concern of the details.'"

—Sharon Dean, author
of *The Barn* and *The Wicked Bible*

The Twin

KEVIN ST. JARRE

Encircle Publications
Farmington, Maine, U.S.A.

Book design and cover design by Deirdre Wait
Cover photographs © Getty Images

Published by:

Encircle Publications
PO Box 187
Farmington, ME 04938

http://encirclepub.com
info@encirclepub.com

For Nylah, the horse-and-Harley-riding poet-farmer novelist, the animal rights activist and rescuer, early-adopter and innovator in the modern off-grid movement. Lover of dogs, tolerant of cats, wrangler of rabbits . . . she of Squam Lake before it was cool, she of the White Mountains before they were full.

Translator's Proem

What follows is my attempt at a translation of a document I was fortunate enough to purchase while on sabbatical, traveling in Afghanistan. The discovery arose out of an unfortunate situation when one evening, after falling a bit deeply into my cups, I found myself in the custody of a most unhelpful handful of Afghan Local Police. Dressed in concrete-grey uniforms topped with what can only be described as cotton kepis, they apparently felt they needed to collect me and the Canadian Forces soldiers with whom I happened to be keeping company.

Earlier, I had wandered from my hotel in search of any honest man who might be able and willing to both provide and consume rye at a rate somewhat comparable with my own. Not an easy thing to find in Afghanistan, but I located an entire squad who fit the bill nicely. They were staying inside an undersized, nondescript house.

It was only after our transport to the local holding cell, a wretched little hole with crude benches for the eleven of us, that the man wearing the name "Dionne" and known as "Clo-fo" to his friends spoke to me of the jar.

"It is very old," he said. "There is some sort of book inside."

I was interested, but suspicious. "Why are you telling me?"

"I thought it might be valuable to you," he said. His smirk made clear that he was not interested in simply giving the jar away.

I leaned in and softly said, "Just having the jar, if it is of any value, is a serious crime here. You can even be executed for stealing antiquities."

Dionne's face darkened, and his smile fell away. "How much will you give me?"

"I have to see it first," I told him.

The next morning, we were released. With a splitting headache, I followed Dionne back to an area not far from the soldiers' crude dining facility. There, we entered a shipping container and moved carefully through items, perhaps crates, draped in canvas.

He said, "I found it in a cave. Tough to get it back here, I'll tell you."

In the rear of the container, Dionne dropped to one knee and pulled back a cover.

There sat a container, the jar, which was browner and less red than terracotta. It was perhaps twenty inches high and half as wide, with a lid. It was cylindrical and quite heavy. There was no glaze; it was rough and had it been exposed to water it clearly would have absorbed a great deal of it. Inside, there were scrolls of linen. I knew I had to purchase these from the young Canadian—I just couldn't let on what they might be worth to me.

"Yes, well, this is somewhat interesting, however the fact that you have opened the jar certainly depreciates the value," I said.

"Why?"

"How am I to know what you have added or removed

from the jar? Not to mention, you have let moisture and other contaminates into it," I said.

He scratched his head and decided to test me. He played an obvious hand. "Fine. If you don't want it, I'll sell it to someone who does."

Had I at least made an offer, he could pretend to be insulted, but I'd not yet mentioned an amount, so I knew it was bluster. At least, I hoped it was. "Go right ahead." I turned to walk out of the container and did not stop on his first word.

"Wait. So, what do you think it's worth?"

I turned back toward him. "I'll give you $100, U.S."

He laughed.

"I might remind you that you have already exposed yourself to risk by telling even one person that you have the jar in your possession," I said. "The next time you return, you might find the ALP lying in wait. You would be tried and executed within weeks of your arrest."

He stopped laughing. "But it has to be worth more than $100."

I stepped closer and looked at the jar, as if struggling with the decision to offer even a cent more. I looked into his face and could see the worry there. "I'll give you $150 for it." I tried to sound irritated and somewhat bored. Perhaps a bit curious, but not the least bit excited.

He looked the jar over once more, decided his dreams of riches were no more than that, sighed and dropped his shoulders. I paid him and lifted the jar, wrapped in its cover, and walked away without another word.

Arriving at my quarters, I immediately locked the door. I set the jar in the middle of the floor. Opening it, I looked inside at the linen, wrapped in a leather thong. I could see the leather tab the thong once passed through, sitting in the bottom of the jar. When I pulled the manuscript out, I was intrigued and assumed that it might be older than 10th century. Perhaps something as exciting as an early Pashto collection, and therefore beyond my ability to read any of it, but still of great value. Instead, to my surprise, I found the work to be written in Koine Greek.

I would normally have immediately turned such a find over to local authorities, but in Afghanistan in those days it seemed a poor choice, and I was clearly better able to understand the import of the find than some bureaucrat one generation removed from herding goats. I attempted to devise a way of secreting the text out of the country but it was impossible. There was only one solution. I had to copy the manuscript. For the rest of my stay, I labored day after day, transcribing the text. Under the circumstances, I am sure I made at least some minor errors but what follows stands as my best effort and certainly better than most could have done. I have also done my best to enhance the text a bit since ancient authors shared so little of what they were feeling that it left the narrative wanting. Also, I have added modest touches here and there, mostly cosmetic, such as an appropriate quotation at the beginning of each section. Of course, as I am a scholar after all, I have included footnotes and translator's notes in order to aid the reader.

As for the original manuscript, I ultimately surrendered it, and even the jar, into the hands of the Ministry of Information and Culture. However, in response to my recent inquiries, the ministry denies ever having received the writings. In fact, they continue to deny any knowledge that such a manuscript ever existed. I am not the least bit surprised and I am only the more grateful that I had the insight and ability to transcribe the document.

What you are about to read is a later draft of a translation I made from the copy I carried out of Afghanistan.

Faithfully submitted,
—B. L. Treah, PhD, Professor of Classics,
University of Cincinnati

I

We must no more ask whether the soul and body are one than ask whether the wax and the figure impressed on it are one.
—Aristotle

I

Among his closest followers there were three of us named Judas. There was the Iscariot. There was also Judas, the younger brother of James, whom we called Taddai as a term of endearment. As for me, I am known as Judas the Twin, or in Aramaic—Tau'ma. I am called Thomas, and perhaps known best for doubt born of grief.[1]

It was winter, my thirteenth year, when they came.[2] Their robes were dyed with pigments such as saffron, creating layers of color on each man ranging from pale gold to a deep red. There were eight monks in all, but there were many more who had traveled with them.

They came to the palace of Herod a year before the king's death. It was in Jerusalem that they met with Herod, and not Jericho as some have claimed. I know because I was there. I worked there as a craftsman, one of many. I saw them entering and I followed. By the time they reached the court, I was more within their group than without.

Appearing before Herod, king of the Jews and son of Antipater, and his ministers, the [indecipherable] of them,

---

1   Didymus in the Greek, still meaning "twin."
2   Vernon puts the birth of Thomas Didymus at A.U.C. 737.

spoke for the group. He spoke in Greek. "I am called Dawa. We have traveled from the east. There was a sign of a birth, a sign in the sky, in the spring before last."[3] His words were a bit clumsy, but his Greek was nearly as good as my own.[4] Herod said nothing. The ministers, courtiers, the crowd altogether, were silent.

"There was a bright light, stars came together. We believe such signs show us the way," Dawa said.

The crowd began to whisper the word, "Magi. Magi." They took these men to be followers of a religion much focused on astrology, however Dawa and his companions were not Magi, nor were they even Persian.

Dawa said, "We seek our spiritual leader, a great holy man. He left us two years ago. We began watching for some sign of where the holy child might be born. The sign appeared and bade us travel west, to your land, before it faded and was gone. It was bright and one among them was red. Do you remember it?"

The stars. I remembered them well, as did we all. A bright rope of stars. However, it had not appeared to our west. The crowd buzzed now, excited. No one spoke directly to Dawa until Herod nodded slightly to one of his ministers, a man named Ptolemaeos. He turned to Dawa and said, "The stars were to our south. They were close. It seemed one could have walked directly beneath them in half a night."

Dawa turned to his companions and whispered something. He then turned back and asked, "Is there a village or town nearby to the south?"

---

3   This would indicate "Star of Bethlehem" event at A.U.C. 748. or 6 B.C.

4   Having read the writer's Greek, I can attest that Dawa's Greek must have been clumsy indeed.

Herod himself suddenly said, "You seek a king." His face was dark, his tone menacing. A chill passed through me.[5] I doubted Dawa understood with whom he was dealing. Herod had killed his own sons and wife out of fear for his throne.

Dawa seemed momentarily confused. "Our guide. We come to find him."

Herod asked, "And his child will be born here?"

Dawa was patient. "Not his child." He paused for a moment, apparently searching his Greek. "The spirit of our holy one would have returned to be born of man on Earth with [indecipherable] in time."

"Why would your holy spirit make pregnant a woman in Judea?" Herod asked.

Dawa frowned and looked back to his fellow travelers. He turned back and said, "Great king. We believe our guide has returned to show us the way."

Herod rose. "There is a village to the south. Bethlehem. Go there and find him. When you discover the child, send me word so that I, too, may adore your newly born leader."

Dawa asked, "Might one of your men come with us, to show us the way to this village?"

Herod's face became grim. I knew that he did not want to send any of his men, because this would have caused fear among those whom the travelers might question. Herod scanned the room until his eyes fell on me.

"Take him with you," Herod said, pointing. All in the

---

5   *I have taken a bit of license here. The original document did indicate Herod's tone was menacing, but it made no mention of Thomas's reaction. I pictured the young craftsman being chilled at said tone and thought I might strengthen the narrative. Please forgive my minor improvements.*

room turned to me. I looked from Herod to Dawa. The latter smiled and nodded slightly. I felt a sudden calm settle upon me.[6] I would take them to Bethlehem.

---

6   *I found nothing to indicate that Thomas was not calm at this moment and, again, I add this line in an attempt to imbue the text with a bit of human emotion.*

2

I walked along with them. Bethlehem was not difficult to find. I did not object to going but I was not sure why they had asked for a guide. One simply needed to walk south on that one road until sunset and he would arrive in Bethlehem. Of course, this group of men, camels, and horses would take longer. They stopped often. None of the men rode the animals, instead walking alongside. The animals carried burdens and pulled carts.

Dawa approached me as we walked. "What do you do for the king?"

"I am a craftsman," I answered.

"In wood?" he asked.

I said, "Mostly stone, there is little wood in this part of Judea. The craftsmen here, homebuilders and tool makers, work with metals and stone."

He did not immediately respond. I was not sure he had understood my Greek until he asked, "How long have you worked in your trade?"

"I began apprenticing at the end of my 7th year," I said.

Dawa was quiet again.

"Are you an astrologer?" I asked. "By trade?"

He said, "I am a student."

"Are you a slow learner?" I asked. He had no hair and no whiskers but the lines in his face betrayed him to be a man of at least forty years.

Dawa laughed. It was a rich sound, unencumbered. The laughter of a child. I hadn't laughed like that since before my apprenticeship began and I would not laugh that way for some years to come.

He said, "I am a slow learner. I believe many of us are slow." His grin was broad. "What do they call you?"

I was not smiling, nor was I offended at his laughing at my question. I was curious. I said, "I am called Judas, the twin. You may call me that. You may call me Thomas."

"Why are you called the twin? Have you a brother?" Dawa asked.

The caravan stopped suddenly. We both looked ahead. There was no obstruction, nothing to impede our progress.

"Why have we stopped again?" I asked.

Dawa answered without looking at me. "Why not stop?"

"Because it will take us well into the night to get to Bethlehem at this rate," I said. "Will we wake the village looking for your king?"

Dawa turned to face me. "Not a king. A guide. Our friend."

"But the child was recently born, how can you know him?" I asked.

Dawa sat on the edge of the road and invited me join him. I looked ahead, saw men casually talking. I sighed and sat.

"We believe that when someone's body dies, his spirit lives on and is reborn into a new life," Dawa said. "Our friend was a very holy man, very special. Soon after he died, we began watching for signs as to where he might next arrive. The signs led us here."

"You believe that the spirit of your dead friend will be inside the child you seek? Like a possession?" I asked.

"Not as two struggling for control of one body. The body will be rightly and solely his," Dawa said.

I paused and then asked, "How will you know the child when you find him?"

"We will give the child an ancient test," Dawa said. His voice sounded calm and sure.

"What will you do with the child?" I asked.

Dawa said, "If we find our friend, we will explain the situation to his mother and father."

"Isn't your friend's spirit the father? You told Herod that the spirit made the woman pregnant," I said.

"I did not say that," Dawa said. "I said only that we believe our guide has returned."

Many of the men were sitting by this time. I wanted to find the child. I said, "I should go ahead and find the child before you arrive. Then I will lead you to him and you can test him."

"Thomas," Dawa said, "let me tell you a story. A man told his son one night, 'Tomorrow we will go to the village and bring something back.' The next morning the son woke very early and without asking any more from his father, set out for the village on his own. When he reached the village, he was already very tired. He also realized that he did not know what his father had intended to bring back from the village. He returned to his father, so hungry and thirsty and exhausted he believed he might die. His father thought him a fool for suffering so much without purpose or accomplishment."

I understood immediately and my face grew hot.[7] I asked,

---

7   *Indicator of embarrassment is my own addition.*

"Why not simply tell me to stay quiet and not go to the village rather than tell me this story to embarrass me?"

Dawa smiled. "Stories reveal their lessons to those who are ready to learn. They also carry their lessons across languages and lifetimes. Whenever you teach, Thomas, try to teach with stories." Dawa stood and walked toward the lead elements of the caravan. The other men rose slowly in response and the caravan began to move again. Being their guide, I thought I should follow.[8]

---

8   *I thought this line, which appeared in the original text, was perhaps too cheeky to include, but I decided in the interest of preserving the integrity of the document to leave it in.*

3

We arrived well after dark. Most villagers went to sleep when the sun set and did not wake until dawn. The streets were empty. We could not see a single lit lamp within any of the homes. Constructed of basalt, the walls of the houses themselves were dark, made of large squared stones, with gaps filled with smaller rocks. Neatly fit and solid. Some houses had two stories.

I was frustrated. We should have been able to arrive much earlier. The lamps we carried did not illuminate much.

Dawa said, "I know it is late."

"We should leave the village and camp outside it until morning," I said.

Dawa said nothing and we continued through the middle of the village. Every one of them searched the stone walls and the wooden doors. There was suddenly a rush of whispers, hushed voices full of excitement. Dawa smiled at me and walked toward the noise. I followed. Arriving, I saw they were standing before the door of a two-story house. Inlaid perfectly in the wood were three stones, arranged vertically. The largest was the highest and white, the second was a small piece of Jerusalem red limestone, the third and bottom stone was also white but half the size of the first.

Dawa turned to me and said, "The sign."

"The stars," I answered.[9]

They were all excited, embracing one another, some in tears. Such rejoicing. I found it compelling.[10]

Dawa stepped forward and called into the house. "We have come a long way. Wake, wake inside."

I scowled. This was incredibly inappropriate. It was entirely possible that there would be no answer from within. It was dark after all and no honest man worked after dark.

Dawa called again. "Wake inside and come to the door."

"I come," a voice said from inside.

When the door opened, an old man met us. I initially thought it might well be the grandfather of the child we sought.

"I am Joseph,[11] what could you want in the night?" he said.

Dawa's voice was steady and low. Perhaps even cautious. "Man. We have traveled for nearly two years, following a path set for us by a sign. We believe our journey may have ended on your doorstep."

"What sign?" Joseph asked. He rubbed his worn face. His hands were enormous and calloused. I recognized the hands of a man who had worked for decades in my own trade. Clearly, he was a craftsman. I took another look at his walls. Very few small stones, few gaps to fill. Skilled for sure,

---

9   *"Stars" my translation of a much longer explanation.*
10   *He must have, although he did not record it.*
11   *Translating 'Yusef' to 'Joseph' just because of the familiarity. Will do the same with most of the other names as well, but I will leave 'Yeshua' as 'Yeshua' as you will soon see. I do this because the very name 'Jesus' is so loaded with such religious weight that it distracts from this narrative.*

patient. A man who took the time to walk and find the next stone, the right stone.

Dawa pointed at the stones inlaid in the wooden door. "That sign. The stars. Is there a child inside born from that time?"

At that moment, there was a cry from inside the house. I felt a flutter across my own skin.[12] The sense that the voice of that child would become so central to my life was unavoidable. I looked up at Dawa who smiled broadly.

"What of the child?" Joseph asked.

"We mean him no harm. We come to adore him. May we enter your house?" Dawa asked.

I watched as Joseph looked out at the strange caravan, the odd clothing, the unfamiliarity of it. He seemed uncertain. He looked at me and I could only stare, holding my breath that he would allow us to see the child.[13]

"Allow them to enter, please, Joseph," said a young woman hidden behind him. She had spoken in Aramaic. Joseph glanced over his shoulder and then back at Dawa.

Joseph said, "I will allow you to enter. Be still and wait." He then closed the door.

Dawa did not take a step but instead sat cross-legged where he was. The others followed his example. I sat as well. I was experiencing a mix of feelings I had never known. Expectation, fear, joy all at once and I had no understanding of why.[14] We saw an oil lamp slowly glow to life within, the olive oil fed from a goatskin suspended from the ceiling.

---

12 Surely his reaction at first hearing the voice of the person he would someday accept as his master.

13 Perhaps not literally holding his breath.

14 Really, the absence of an explanation as to how Thomas felt during all this is a distraction I can only hope I have adequately remedied.

I asked Dawa, "How will you test the child?"

"You will see soon enough," he said.

"You will test him right away?"

"It is why we have come," he said.

The door opened. Dawa and five of the men went inside. I followed. Joseph stood by the door. Across the room, on a small bench, sat a woman who [indecipherable]. Joseph said, "My wife, Miriam."

Clearly, she was an Essene, very modest in her dress, but the family room was quite large, the kitchen beyond well appointed with jars and plenty of food hung from the ceiling.[15] Upon her knee sat a young boy, hair tussled. He was no longer crying, he only sat and stared.

"This is Yeshua," she said in Aramaic.

I translated for Dawa. "His name is Iesous."

Dawa and the others approached slowly. One carried a bundle of cloth. They opened it. Within there were a great many items. Toys of wood, a string of silver bells, a small knife, a gold cup, a head carved of stone, a bronze bowl. They laid the cloth out flat and spread the items evenly.

Dawa said to Miriam, "Please allow your son to choose." I translated this into Aramaic, but she nodded before I finished. She understood the Greek, but perhaps was not comfortable speaking it.

She put Yeshua down and whispered into his ear. The child

---

15   *The original document obviously did not use the term "Essene" but I use it here since it is true to the tone used by the author to describe Miriam. Additionally, it is widely accepted that the Mary character from Christianity was an Essene. Finally, it would fit perfectly that strangers would come looking for a special child and, finding a child of this particular ascetic sect which believed so fiercely in the nearing end times and a coming messiah, would find a mother willing in her mysticism to believe so much based on so little.*

smiled and walked onto the cloth, straight to the gold cup. He lifted it with both hands and ran back to his mother. A moan rose from Dawa and his men. They fell to their knees and prostrated themselves before the boy. Joseph appeared concerned but Miriam had an arm around her son and both had a look of complete peace on their faces, the heavy cup held low by them both.

"Is it him?" I asked.

Dawa sat back on his heels. "It is. That cup belonged to our friend and master. We have found him."

Two of the men went out and returned with two [indecipherable]. One contained the resin of guggal and the other the dried plaster daindhava.[16]

"What was the name of your friend?" I asked as the gifts were presented at Miriam's feet.

Dawa smiled and looked at me. "He is Gyalwa Nagarjuna."

I frowned. Who could manage such a name? "Do you have to use that name? Does he?"

"No," Dawa said. "He can choose any name he likes." Dawa then spoke directly to Miriam. "Gifts for you. You are highly favored, our guide and leader has come to you."

Miriam looked at Yeshua and, momentarily, concern flashed across her face.

Dawa continued, saying, "Do not be afraid, Miriam, you have found great favor. You conceived and gave birth to a son, you have called him Yeshua. He has been, is, and will be a great man. A leader and guide for many."

Miriam looked to Joseph, who only stared at Yeshua.

"Let me try to explain. The spirit of our guide has come to you, to your womb. We believe that life is lived again and

---

16 n.b. the word "plaster" here might well have been better translated as "gum"

again, and that his life, leadership, and guidance is without end," Dawa said.

"How can this be?" Miriam responded, in Aramaic. "I have been touched by no spirit." I did my best to translate for Dawa but these words such as 'spirit'… what would be the best interpretation?[17] I was a craftsman, after all, and not a priest. Still, Dawa seemed to understand.

"It was not an event to be perceived, but even that which we cannot see can come to pass," Dawa said.

"An act of God?" Miriam asked.

Joseph spoke to her in Aramaic, "Anything is possible for God, behold even your cousin Elisabeth, though all thought her barren in her old age, has a son."

Miriam spoke to Joseph, "But what do they want with him? Do they want to take Yeshua?"

"Dawa, she is concerned that you want to take the boy away," I said.

Dawa raised both hands. "The boy will stay here until he is a man."

I quickly translated but again Miriam had understood.

Dawa said, "We will leave without him. When the boy is older, we will return and invite him to come with us, to study in the mountains where he has lived so many times before. We would never compel anyone to go or stay. Each must find his own path."

Joseph said nothing. He stepped closer to Miriam, if only to show his support. It was clear to me how fond he was of her.

Miriam paused a moment, and then in broken Greek said, "I am God's servant. Let him be with me and when he is a man, when you return, we will discuss."

---

17   *Ah, the burdens of translation.*

Dawa smiled in agreement and turned to his party. They had waited patiently. They spoke in hushed tones. I looked at Yeshua. Or Gyalwa Nagarjuna. The boy was standing, cup at his feet, his hands on Miriam's knee. He rocked back and forth. I looked at the visitors and could see their train outside. How had this little boy brought all this attention? I could feel my life shift beneath my feet. A new path was opening in front of me.

"Dawa, when you depart, may I come with you?" I asked. My words surprised only me. Dawa calmly nodded my way and then returned to talking with his colleagues. I had no family, nothing to hold me, and my trade was of use anywhere. I was an adult. Still, I was surprised at my impulsiveness. I knew nothing of these visitors, of their land, of their ways, and yet I was to follow them.

Another boy walked out from a different room, rubbing his eyes. He took in the visitors and moved quickly to Joseph. He was only a few years older than Yeshua and he embraced Joseph's leg.

Dawa faced Miriam and Joseph once more. Joseph said, "This is my son, James. His mother died some years ago. My daughters still sleep."[18]

Dawa waved at James as a child might and the boy hid his face. Yeshua was not shy and walked directly to Dawa and tugged on his robe. Dawa went to his knees before the boy. Yeshua smiled broadly and embraced Dawa. I must say it was a moment I will never forget.[19]

---

18   n.b. there can be no mistake here, the words are "son" and "daughters" as in the familial and not in the mystical sense.

19   I am quite sure he might have thought something to this effect.

4

When we left Joseph's house, we camped outside the village. I did not sleep well. I dreamed of Herod, of the sons whom he had killed or let Rome kill. There had been something in Herod's voice. He was old and infirm but I was still frightened and my dreams were of many horrors. When the sun rose, I was watching it. Dawa approached before I [indecipherable] and I told him of my dreams and how Herod had left precious few of his potential heirs alive.

Dawa stared eastward. "We will not tell Herod what we have learned. We will return a different way."

"We will not be safe anywhere within sight of Rome," I said.[20]

"We will return a different way," Dawa repeated.

"What of the child?" I asked.

Dawa said, "Return to the family, tell them of your dreams. They may travel with us, as far as they like."

"Which way will we go?" I asked.

"We came by way of Damascus. Let us leave by Egypt and

then the sea," he said. "Tell them we will be in Bethlehem before midday."

*   *   *

When I came to Joseph's house, I found him outside shaping a stone with both boys watching intently. As I approached, he saw me but never paused in his work.

"Dawa sent me. He and his party will be here at midday. They will be returning to their homeland. They wish you to know that you and your family may travel with them as far as you would like," I said.

James considered me closely, but Joseph did not look at me. "Why would we leave?"

I spoke slowly. "I had troubled dreams in the night. Of Herod. He asked Dawa to inform him when the child had been found."

Joseph looked up at this. "Has he sent word to Herod?"

"They intend to leave by a different route in an effort to hide the child but they, and I, am concerned. I believe you should bring your family and whatever you may and follow them as far as you care to." I watched the man think this over. He was older, with at least four children, and a wife. He had a home, with food, and a concern that seemed to be successful. He would leave all this on the invitation of strangers and on account of my dreams?

Yeshua stepped forward. "We should go." Before these words, I had not even known the child could speak.

And so it was. When Dawa and the others arrived, Joseph had packed the tools of his craft, much of the family's clothing, and some provisions into a small cart drawn by a beast.[21] I had some concern that Joseph would be angry with Dawa for bringing this trouble to his family, but Joseph was completely at peace.

"We meant only to find Gyalwa Nagarjuna," Dawa said, an apology of sorts I thought.

Joseph said, "If it is the will of God that we flee, then we flee. I trust in Him. I trust that He has sent you to us."

"You are welcome to return to the mountains with us," Dawa said.

"I will keep my eyes and ears open and He will instruct me," Joseph replied.

It seemed to me that Dawa admired Joseph his sensitivity and openness to the larger[22], no matter what either man called it. I admired them both. I also had a problem.

"I cannot go with you, not immediately," I said.

Dawa said nothing; his eyes locked with mine, he waited.

"I will be missed in the morning. I am expected. They will wonder where I am, where you are. They may even begin to search. I must go back to the palace, to the work. I will tell them that you have yet to find the child and that you continue to search. I will thus achieve time for you to make your escape. Perhaps two days," I said.

"You may not be able to rejoin us," Joseph said.

"I will wait two days and then I will try." I thought Joseph was probably correct.

Dawa said, "There are two roads. One goes through Gaza, but we would be less safe that way. We must take the road through Hebron but then on to Bersabe, not Gaza. Once

---

21   *The text did not read "beast" per se, but I could not discern what sort of animal it was. It was something akin to "self-bearer." More than likely, an ass.*

22   *The "larger" in a spiritual sense, in an energetic sense, perhaps.*

there, we will get provisions enough to cross the desert and then on to the sea."

Turning to me, Joseph said, "Miriam has a cousin in Hebron, Elisabeth wife of Zacharias. Seek her out. She will give you word of our [indecipherable] and feed you." To Dawa he said, "You know our land well."

Dawa said, "We have excellent maps. In this lifetime, I have never been this far."

"I will follow, and I will do as you say," I said. I was afraid.[23] It would take days to walk that far.

"If we can, if it feels safe, we will wait for you for up to two days in Bersabe. If you leave when you say you will, you may find us rested, provisioned, and ready to depart," Dawa said.

I looked at Yeshua. His face was placid. Miriam approached me. She placed her hand on my shoulder. I meant to shrug it off since I was no longer a boy, but had recently achieved manhood. She herself could not have been more than three or four years my senior. However, I could not. Such peace washed through my heart, I could not bear to pull from her touch. It was the first of two occasions in my life when the woman, the mother of Yeshua, would touch me, and on both occasions, I was left feeling powerless. I looked into her soft dark eyes.[24] She smiled, removed her hand, and then stepped away.

I looked at Joseph and then to Dawa. "I will try to get for you the two days." Dawa stepped forward and took me in a

---

23 *He must have been.*

24 *The reader will forgive me my indulgences. This was just such a potentially poignant moment, I could not resist, as I am sure any true scholar would understand. The text actually indicates only that she touched his shoulder.*

full embrace. He released me and I was scarcely clear of his arms when I took my first step toward Jerusalem. I did not look back.

5

The next morning, I approached the Nicanor Gate. The paving stones of the temple courtyard were four cubits long by three cubits wide and alternated in color from a dark brown to a pale.[25] The bottom steps to the gate were long and the subsequent ones rose in concentric stone curves each stacked on the last. I had been working with other young craftsmen under the guidance of a master named Menelaus on these very steps. Curving a stone was not especially challenging but cutting stone to these exacting specifications required more than a steady hand and instead a great deal of planning and calculation before one reached for the chisel. I knew that I would not be able to concentrate on that particular day, however, and my anxiety only increased.

"Thomas, you are early," Menelaus said as I arrived at the steps. He was kind, patient, and incredibly generous with his time. It had been almost thirty years since he had been an apprentice, but he seemed to remember exactly what it was like. There were blocks arranged and tools set neatly about, waiting for the others to arrive.

---

25 *Best approximation of colors.*

"I am," I said. I had never been this early before. I had never been the first to arrive. I could not begin to work alone. I could not sit in full view of the master, especially since he remained on his feet. So I stood, awkwardly.

Having worked for him and learned from him for nearly three years at that point, I believe Menelaus knew something was amiss. He asked, "Are you ill?"

"I am not," I said.

He considered me for a moment and then asked, "What of the strangers you led to Bethlehem?"

"I left them there," I said. I did not want to lie to him. He pressed no further. Another of the apprentices arrived, a boy in his first year named Telemachus. He surveyed the day's work ahead of us. Menelaus was studying me and I waited for him to ask another question about Dawa and the child. He did not.

Menelaus said, "You two begin on the far end, but before you cut the stone, scribe it and prove it to me."

We both nodded and got to work. The others arrived in due time and my day took shape as had so many before. We focused on calculations and shaping. Fitting and refitting. The slightest flaw and we withdrew the stone. If need be, we would cast the stone aside but as the day wore on, each stone increased in value by the amount of labor poured into it, and after a few hours a single stone could become dear indeed.

I noticed as the sun dipped toward the horizon that Menelaus was talking with someone behind the columns off to the right. I could not see with whom, only an additional shadow lying between those of the columns. As the other departed, Menelaus turned and strode toward me. His face was set and grim. Truly, I thought I had angered the man. If only I had been right. He walked past me without stopping but seized my upper arm in the iron grip of a well-seasoned stonemason. I stumbled after him as he led me into a dark corner, away from the others.

"What have you done? Those whom you led to Bethlehem, they have departed. No one is sure of their route, but they did not come back to inform Herod. He is in a rage," Menelaus said. His fingers dug deep into my arm.

"What of it? What has it to do with me? I do not know where they have gone," I said. I hoped I could be convincing on this point.

"For the time being, Herod is less concerned with where the strangers have gone," Menelaus said. His eyes shifted back and forth, seeming to search mine for something.

"What is it?" I asked.

"He is afraid that a challenger to his heirs has been born. In Bethlehem. These travelers have Herod convinced that a future king was born nearly two years ago," he said.

I waited. Somewhere in my heart, I believe I knew what he would say next.[26]

"Herod has ordered the death of every boy, near two years of age, in Bethlehem," Menelaus said.

His words struck me, but not with enough force to set me free from his grasp. I twisted and pulled. He would not release me.

"Let go of me!" I said.

"What will you do? It will not be safe!"

I brought both my feet up and kicked at him. I was like a child in a father's grasp. I managed only to throw myself to the ground with one arm still in his grip.

---

26 *Flourish mine.*

"Release me at once!" I said.

"You can do nothing!"

I thought I might never get free of him until his face hardened and he suddenly released me without another word. I went off as quickly as I could manage and ran a good portion of the way to Bethlehem.

When I arrived, Herod's soldiers were dragging boys out of their homes, out of the arms of their mothers. In the center of Bethlehem, not far from Joseph's home, they collected them. I joined many of the parents in forming a large ring around the dozen soldiers who had formed a perimeter around the boys. The soldiers held out their swords, pointing them at us. Some of the children cried for their parents, others waved, still others simply sat. One little boy who looked a great deal like Yeshua simply walked in a small circle. I pleaded with the nearest soldier for the release of the boys and I was struck to the ground.

When the patrol collecting the boys returned to the center with one last child, their number was complete. Every boy of Bethlehem younger than two years of age was inside the ring of soldiers. All together, there were eight boys. More quickly than it could be comprehended, four soldiers inside the perimeter raised their swords and each cut down two of the boys. All eight were struck dead in that moment.[27]

I screamed, my own voice lost in the wail of the parents as they surged forward. A few were run through by the perimeter soldiers, but nearly all collapsed when they

---

27   It is indeed significant that the number of innocents murdered has apparently been greatly exaggerated throughout the centuries. This firsthand account I have discovered and brought to light must certainly be henceforth the new definitive source on this incident.

comprehended the enormity and finality of what they had seen. A woman fell across the backs of my legs and I was momentarily pinned there. A soldier stepped on my hand as they then unceremoniously withdrew, leaving the pile of little bleeding corpses to the devastated parents.

The soldiers marched away, toward Jerusalem, back to Herod. I felt such rage, such hate. The woman crawled off my legs and toward her dead child. I watched and was ill.[28]

I turned from the sight and ran south, meaning to immediately strike out and find Dawa and Joseph and the others, but then realized that someone might notice my flight out of Bethlehem in the opposite direction from whence I had come. Someone might follow and I would betray where Yeshua had gone. I stopped at Joseph's house, looked behind me once more, and pushed my way inside.

I planned to wait until dark. There was no hope of sleep. Instead, I wept. Curled on the floor, I wept. Little hands. All I could remember were small, upraised hands, attempting to fend off swords. It was then that the door was first struck and I heard the voices.

I went to a [indecipherable][29] and I could see them. Grief-mad. A crowd of the parents of the slain boys, some carrying their bloody children in their arms.

"Open the door, Joseph!" a man shouted.

Another said, "Your son was not among the boys, your Yeshua was spared! We want to know why!"

"Was it the strangers? Did your strangers bring this to us?" shrieked a woman. She was the potteress; I had seen her

---

28   In the text, he indicated he was ill, however the feelings of rage expressed two sentences earlier were my interpretation of how he surely must have felt.

29   Some sort of window, I assume

at her work. Her hands, so recently in clay, were covered in drying blood.

I did not know what to do. At not finding Joseph and Yeshua, what would they do with me? I decided to remain quiet, hoping they would leave. They did not. The shouts and cries only grew louder, more intense. They were throwing large stones at the house. They did not care if anyone was inside or not. The house had become a sink for their grief and anger and madness and I was inside. I knew they would want to tend to their dead before sunset, but I knew the well-made walls would not keep them out that long. The anticipation, along with the roar, only grew. I clutched my ears and shouted along with them, my own voice lost in the cacophony, until the door finally failed. When it did, it was almost a relief. They streamed in and had filled the room before they noticed me. They smashed benches and threw down what Joseph had not taken with them.

A large man found me against the wall and lifted me to my toes. Before I could say a word, a woman struck me in the head with a small rock she had carried in with her. The crowd surged around me. I was convinced that I would be promptly killed. The man had asked me three times before I heard him.

"Where is Joseph?"

I shook my head.

"There is no food in the house, no clothing. They fled. How did they know the soldiers would come?" another man asked.

I shook my head again.

"Speak! Say something!"

I said, "I do not know where they have gone. I do not know them."

"Lies! I have seen you before!"

I nodded. "I was there, I saw what they did. I ran in here out of fear."

"You are not from here, not from Bethlehem. You came with the soldiers?" a man asked.

I knew that I could not say I had come from Jerusalem and not be associated with the monsters[30] that had murdered their sons, least of all tell them I came from Herod's palace.

"No," I said. "I did not come with them."

"You were here, the other day," said a woman, her eyes swollen. "You were here, with the strangers."

"I was not here," I said.

A grumbling grew among them.

"You know Joseph. You came here. You know of his son, Yeshua."

"I do not know Yeshua," I said. I felt a strange flush of guilt at this, as if denying the boy was wrong.[31]

The man holding me shook me violently. "Do not lie to us, boy!"

"I am not lying!" I said. "I came to the village to find work and instead saw the tragedy befall your sons. I fled and hid in this house. That is all I know!"

The grumbling grew louder.

"He lies! He brought the soldiers!"

I was convinced I was not going to survive this time in Bethlehem until I heard his voice.

"Release him."

Everyone stopped, fell silent, and looked as Menelaus entered and approached.

---

30   *Perhaps better translated as "terrors"*

31   *This is reasonably close and I thought it interesting to foreshadow the tale of Simon "Peter's" thrice denying knowing Jesus on the night of the crucifixion.*

"Who are you?" a man shouted.

"I am a craftsman, this is my son. He had nothing to do with your sorrow today. We only came to this region seeking work. Release him. He is innocent, just as your children were. See to them, see to the rites. Go and weep as families, do not add more blood to this day."

The intensity of the crowd shifted from rage to a purer grief at Menelaus's words. Still, the large man had not released me. Menelaus came to us and slowly seized the man's wrist in a grip I knew all too well. It was not unlike having one's arm trapped beneath a large stone. The man's face twisted from anger, to pain, to grief. The man released me and Menelaus released him.

Menelaus turned to the crowd. "See to your dead sons. Perform the rites. Go and be with one another."

6

I set out that evening. Menelaus had agreed that I could not return to Jerusalem. He prevented me from telling him where I was going or why or with whom, saying what he did not know he could not divulge. He warned me to be wary out on the road at night. We embraced and parted ways.

Sticking to the way, it was approximately eighteen miles[32] to Hebron from Bethlehem. It was not an easy journey, even in daytime. Hebron is set in the hills, the terrain is rocky. In the dark, walking is treacherous, even without bandits. The night air was cold. I was exhausted by the time I had traveled perhaps half the distance. Up ahead, just off the road, was a fire. How I wanted to sit beside those flames and warm myself.[33] Still, I had to be cautious. Only someone without fear would build such a fire. A wary traveler would set up camp and be sleeping somewhere off the road, without a fire and with little sign of his presence. The fire ahead could be seen for miles and was very close to the road.

I approached carefully. Seeing no one, I circled the fire just

---

32 *Some help here from the translator.*
33 *It is safe to assume this much.*

outside of its glow. No one. No beast, no [indecipherable][34] but bread and a jar perhaps of water or wine. Had someone abandoned a fire of this size? I looked in all directions, out into the dark, impossible to see the fire still in my eyes. Was it a trap? Set a large fire with food and drink and move into the shadows to wait for a traveler who might be robbed? Elaborate when one could just as easily be robbed on the road. In my thirst, I approached the fire and reaching the jar, found clean-smelling water. I drank and quenched my thirst. No sooner had I put down the jar did he arrive and speak to me.

"Eat," he said.

I rose. He bade me sit. I did so.

"Eat," he said. "You still have a long way to Hebron."

I asked, "How do you know where I am going?"

"You are on the road to Hebron." His voice was kind but false and so familiar. "Eat."

"I am not hungry," I said. This was not true.

"Twin, eat, you might not eat again until Bersabe. What if the house in Hebron is empty?" he said.

I did not move. "Why are you here?"

"I know you and I know your purpose. I know, too, that they do not trust you."

I wanted to ask, "Who?" but I said nothing. I knew that he knew.

"They do not trust you," he said. "They go to Gaza. You will find yourself alone in Bersabe."

Was this true? I suddenly had doubt.[35] What if I found myself in Bersabe and then set out into the desert trying to

---

34   *Cloth or garment or blanket, perhaps?*
35   *I trust the reader will forgive my foreshadowing the doubt for which he will be so famous.*

catch Dawa while he had gone on to Gaza and then to sea?

His voice filled my ears. "Eat."

I rose. "I will not eat. I will go on to Hebron and then to Bersabe. While they provision themselves, I will catch them there. We will go on from there together."

He followed and gripped my heart and said, "I warn you now that the child will bring you to much misery and sadness. He will take your life from you."

I tried to distance myself, but his grip was more powerful than Menelaus's and so different. He gripped my mind. How I wished my old master were there.[36]

"Release me, sewer[37] of doubt!" I said and he went silent. The pause made it seem that he was considering me for a moment. He then faded. As he entered the shadows, he said, "You still may eat. You will need your strength." He was consumed by the black. This truly had been him.[38] The fire fell and died, a large blaze to embers and then dark ash. I could not walk on and my legs failed and I sat for a time. I wondered if that voice would return. When I found my feet, I abandoned the food and the remaining water and set out for Hebron once more.

I wondered what I might find in Hebron and marveled at how slowly time passed before dawn broke. When I arrived, I climbed to the cave of Machpelah. My thirst was great but before water, I felt compelled to stand at the low wall

---

36   *It is only natural to assume Thomas would have wanted Menelaus to protect him, so I add it here.*

37   *Here, one who sews, but the double entendre is clever, if I do say so myself.*

38   *The text is no more informative than this, but a reader may assume the worst. It is disappointing that a firsthand account of such an encounter is not more developed in its exposition but such is the case with much of ancient writing.*

and stare into the enclosure. While the top of the wall rose only to my ribs, it was thicker than I was tall. There was no door, no way to enter, to approach closer the resting place of Abraham, Isaac, Jacob, and their wives. I raised my hands silently and prayed. Not for a spouse, as so many did here, but for faith and protection. Many stared and watched me, dirty and tired as I looked. I prayed until I fell.[39]

In time, I went down into the market at the edge.[40] I had little money, only a few lepton and prutah. I was not even sure if my prutah would be accepted here. A small stand held loaves and figs and other foodstuffs. A man and beautiful girl stood fast by.

I said to the man, "I have a question."

"I have only what you see," he said.

"I want to know where I might find the home of Zacharias and his wife Elisabeth," I said.

"The old priest?" he asked.

"I am sent by her cousin."

He looked at me, suspicion on his face. "So you are more interested in his wife."

"I was told she would feed me," I said. My mouth watered at the goods before me, and my thirst was unspeakable.

He grunted at me and adjusted his wares. The girl stepped forward and said, "The priest and his wife and child live an hour's walk that way." She pointed generally into the hills and my heart sank.

"Might I have a drink?" I asked.

"Pay?" the man asked.

"I have these prutah," I said. I did not reveal all I had for

---

39   *It is unclear what happened here. Perhaps from thirst and fatigue.*

40   *Of the village, one assumes.*

fear of how thirsty I might look.

"Prutah!" he said.

The girl extended her arms with a vessel[41] and the man hissed at her. Still, she did not flinch and I drank. After, she refused my payment and he stepped away. I thanked her and set out for the home of the priest.

---

41 *The original word was an obscure one, perhaps slang, but one can assume it was some sort of vessel, after all.*

7

When I arrived at the house of Zacharias, I announced, "Peace to all within." I was greeted by the usual [indecipherable][42] and it was good. They knew how I was called and that I would come.

Here was a child half a year older than Yeshua, and wilder in his aspect. How he climbed and ran about! I could not help but think of the eight boys murdered in Bethlehem just the day before.[43]

"His name is John," Elisabeth said.

Zacharias smiled and lifted the child. He said, "And you, boy, you will be called the Prophet of The Most High, for you will go before the Lord's representative that you may prepare his way so that he may give knowledge to his people so that their sins may be forgiven in God's mercy, which Yeshua will bring to enlighten those who sat in the dark and in death's shadow, so that he may direct our feet on the path of contentment."

---

42 *This part of the document was not damaged or illegible, it was simply indecipherable. I doubt any translator could have managed any better than I. I will use this wherever it occurs throughout the manuscript.*

43 *Of course he would think of those boys, so I add it here.*

I found this odd.[44] I asked, "Why do you think Yeshua is special? Is it because of Dawa and the others? And do you believe in a path to contentment?"

Elisabeth said, "Long before those travelers came, when I was with child, Miriam came to visit me. She entered our house just as you did, invoking peace. When I heard the greeting, the baby in my womb leapt and I was filled with a Spirit of Holiness."

"A spirit?" I asked.

Elisabeth continued. "In a loud voice, I cried out to Miriam, 'You are blessed among women and blessed is the fruit of your womb. That the mother of my Lord comes to me? When I heard your voice, the baby in my womb leaped for joy. Blessed is she who believed that there would be fulfillment of those things that were said to her in the presence of the Lord.' And then we embraced."

"What did she reply?" I asked.

Elisabeth said, "She says, 'My soul exalts the Lord Jehovah and my spirit rejoices in God my Savior for he has regarded the lowliness of his handmaiden, for behold, from this hour all generations will ascribe blessedness to me because he who is mighty has done unto me great things and holy is his name. His mercy for posterity is upon those who revere him. He has wrought victory with his arm and he has scattered the proud with the opinion of their heart. He has cast down the mighty from thrones and has raised up the lowly. He has filled the hungry with good things and the rich he has sent away empty-handed. He has helped Israel his servant and he has remembered his mercy. Just as he spoke with our Patriarchs, with Abraham and with his seed eternally.'"

---

44 *No doubt Thomas would.*

I then said, "I am surprised to keep learning that it is not Dawa alone who believes this child, Yeshua, to be special. Why would the Lord favor the son of Joseph and Miriam so?"

"Because," Zacharias said, "it is by the hand of the Lord that Miriam conceived, just as it was his blessing that John was sent to us."

"Neither his blessings nor his mercy were with the mothers and sons of Bethlehem," I said.

Zacharias asked, "Why do you say so?"

"Soon the streets and markets will be filled with the news. Herod, in an attempt to kill the child Dawa sought out, to kill Yeshua, has had murdered every boy of Bethlehem younger than two years of age," I said.

Elisabeth asked, "You saw this?"

"I was there."

Zacharias asked, "Is that why you are a day early?"

"I came directly, after nearly being killed myself by the grieving mothers and fathers," I said.

"Such sadness," Elisabeth said, pulling John to her suddenly, the boy wild and resisting.

"So, I am not as confident that there is a path to happiness," I said.

"Contentment and happiness[45] are not the same," he said. "When I was a boy, I heard a man in Damascus speak of a path that would lead away from suffering. A path to contentment. I believe that Yeshua has been chosen to teach his people the way."

I pondered this for a moment and then glanced at Elisabeth. "Priest, I would talk with you separately," I said.

---

45   n.b. this sort of nuanced translation is quite challenging.

We rose and Zacharias said nothing and led me away from the house. We spoke as we walked.

"There is more. On the way to your home, in the night, I stopped by a large fire and was tempted to eat and drink, and drink I did, by one I have known who came to me from a dark place. He[46] told me to abandon Yeshua and his family. He told me that the boy would bring me misery and that, in any case, Dawa and Joseph did not trust me," I said.

Zacharias stopped, but did not look at me.

"He said that they would go to Gaza and go by sea, without leaving me notice, so that I might pursue them on a poor [indecipherable] and lose my way and perish for lack of provisions," I said.

Zacharias said, "No one spoke of a mistrust for you. In truth, at my suggestion that they chance going to Gaza instead, it was Yeshua who insisted they must all wait for you in Bersabe. It seemed important to the boy."

I said, "What could the boy want with me? He hardly knows me. Yeshua is so young, he would in time forget we had ever met."

Zacharias said, "I am careful now with my doubt. He struck me dumb once and I will not do it again. It is you who must trust. Yeshua will wait for you."

"But what of the words of the one who came to me at the fire?" I asked.

"His words are insignificant in the eyes of the Lord who could crush him like a locust beneath a heel. Trust in the good, ask for the Lord's help, and trust in that. You are part of the plan, and Yeshua seems to think an important part at that."

---

46   *Actually, here the text used the neuter form of the pronoun, but as I have done all along, I corrected the grammar.*

I paused a moment and considered my options.[47] "Should I set out immediately and catch them? When did they leave?"

"They are less than half a day ahead of you. Come and eat with us at least. We will prepare you," Zacharias said.

We returned to the house. We sat and ate. Bread dipped in olive oil, grapes, and fresh meat from a recently slaughtered kid.

At some point,[48] Elisabeth asked, "Where is your family?"

"I have no one," I said. "No reason to stay. I have a trade and I will bring it with me."

She opened her mouth once more, as if to speak, but did not. I imagine that she was about to inquire as to why I was known as "the twin" while claiming to have no family, but she said nothing.[49]

We finished our meal without much more being said by anyone. Zacharias had a bundle[50] prepared for me containing bread and dates. Also, he gave me water to carry. I thanked them both for their hospitality and headed out to catch Dawa, Yeshua, and the others. I had nearly twice as far to travel this time, but I knew I could make quicker progress than Dawa's party. I set off for Bersabe.

---

47   *A portion of the manuscript here was simply illegible. What certainly is safe to assume is that he would have been attempting to make some sense of what was happening to him.*

48   *Unsure of when in the course of the meal.*

49   *I imagine he would imagine this, and so I add this here.*

50   *A close approximation.*

8

As I walked I stumbled on a stone and fell. When I rose, he had returned. His voice was as insistent as it had been at the fire on the road to Hebron.

He spoke into my ear.[51] "They are even now leaving Bersabe, they are going to Gaza. There is no way to catch them. Abandon this as they have abandoned you."

"I will do as I said. If they have not done as they have promised, that is beyond my control. I will trust," I said.

"But why do you believe?" he asked.

"What would you have me do?" I asked. "Would you have me return to Jerusalem?"

"Return to Hebron. There is a great deal of work for you in Hebron. The girl who gave you to drink, you found her desirable. Your flesh wanted hers. Return to Hebron and make a life for yourself. Shape stone, come home to her warmth, have children, grow old," he said. His voice was engaging.

I was very tempted.[52] "Give me peace," I told him.

---

51   *The original read that he spoke into "kephale," so one can assume into the ear here.*

52   *He must have been.*

"Even if you catch Yeshua, your life will never be your own. Before your end, you will become his property, and he will even sell you to a stranger from a faraway land. Yeshua is not even of Joseph's blood; she was with child when he found her," he said.

"How would you know all this? Rumors? Gossip from the grief-stricken people of Bethlehem? If I become his servant, then he may do as he wishes, no matter his parentage," I said. "As I said, I will trust."

"But do you even believe in God?" he asked. "Do you truly believe?"

"I believe you exist," I said. "I have proven that I am a man who has faith[53] when others do not. I will prove it again."

At this, he left me. I walked until I slept, rose and walked again. I saw no one until the outskirts of Bersabe, when I spotted some boys on a height, and I thought they hardly noticed me except they stopped their play and stood motionless as I passed. They watched as one might watch a madman come into camp.

Once in Bersabe, I went straight to the market. I thought if Dawa and the others were still provisioning as promised, I would catch them. If not, I might learn where they had gone. As it turned out, I arrived at the market as the men were loading the beasts with the goods they had purchased.

I saw Yeshua before I saw Joseph. The boy walked to me and smiled.

"Where is your father?" I asked but before he could answer, Joseph appeared walking beside Dawa.

"We will part ways then," Joseph said.

"Agreed," said Dawa.

---

53   *Perhaps "...a man who believes..."*

"Part ways?" I asked. "Why? Where will you go?"

Joseph said, "My family and I will go through Gaza to Egypt."

I said, "Herod will know if you go to Gaza. He will get word."

"By the time word gets back to him, we will be beyond Gaza and living inside Egypt," Joseph said.

Dawa said, "If you might go to Alexandria, there are people there who might shelter you, people who will understand the nature of the search which brought me to you, friends of ours." He swept his hand toward his countrymen at this.

I turned to Dawa. "And we will still travel through the desert?"

Dawa said, "We will."

"And board a ship for your homeland?"

Dawa said, "Across the seas and into the mountains."

I thought for a moment and then asked, "Will I be welcomed there?"

Dawa smiled. "You already are. How is it you have caught us so quickly?"

"Herod learned that you had left," I said. "He sent soldiers and the young boys of Bethlehem were murdered."

There was silence. Joseph's face was pained, as I am sure he felt for the neighbors he had left behind.

"I am sorry. I feel I brought this upon you," I said.

"Nothing has happened that was not part of His plan," Joseph said. "Herod will not find Yeshua if God does not wish it so, just as you will not without God's help."

From behind me, I heard his voice. Yeshua said, "Will you come find me?"

I turned and his eyes locked with mine and I had such a feeling. I approached him. I knelt. "I will find you. When you become a man, I will return to Jerusalem and begin to look for you. I promise."

He smiled, as did I.

Miriam stepped forward and stood behind Yeshua. "And you will be welcomed when you return."

"I do not know where we will be in the years to come," Joseph said to Dawa.

Dawa also smiled and said, "You will be where you are."

Joseph did not smile, but instead simply turned and signaled to his family that it was time. Without another word from Miriam or any of the children, they left with their belongings and beasts.

Dawa reached toward me and laid his hand upon my shoulder. "Now that you are here, we will buy the last of our provisions and leave at once."

We began our walk to the sea, with the other men and the many [indecipherable]. Dawa's journey had been a success. My journey was just beginning. I left my world behind and set out toward enlightenment.

II

It is not the oath that makes us believe the man,
but the man the oath.
—Aeschylus

Translator's Notes

The text was nearly silent on the journey, the intervening years, and the return trip to Jerusalem, although it appears that when Thomas did return, he traveled by land. What little was written about Thomas's time in the East, I choose to withhold at this point in the translation simply so that the reader might first experience the region in the text to follow in subsequent chapters. So, this narrative picks up once more with Thomas already in Jerusalem, some ten years later, in search of Yeshua.

Rather than roaming throughout the countryside looking for the family, after arriving in Jerusalem, Thomas let it be known that he had returned and was hoping that Yeshua and his family would come to him in the city. Thomas then patiently waited. This method was successful. The family came to Jerusalem where Thomas and Yeshua met again.

9

How at once grand and drab Jerusalem seemed to me. With Herod years dead, there was certainly a different sense. I could trace my hand over stone that my friends[54] and I had once shaped beneath our master's watchful eye. We had been skilled enough, but we shaped the stone without knowing. Even the Greeks, whose work informed the technique of the east in their portrayals of Gautama Buddha, did not see the Buddha in the stone. As I waited for Yeshua and his family, I hoped one day he would see.

What could I have known of the child? He may very well have rejected it all outright, however I was obligated to learn what the boy would do. I would stay, just as we must all return and return to the craving until every mortal sees the light.

I had learned much during my time in the mountains, and was eager to see if Yeshua would choose to follow the same path. Dawa had not come. I promised him that I would encourage the boy to follow and Dawa had replied, "I will not wait. I am not even certain that you will return. We will see what happens."[55]

---

54 *Loosely translated*
55 *More literally, the text read, "...what may grow."*

When Yeshua and his family arrived, I saw that Joseph had aged considerably and walked with difficulty. It was clear that his final years of craftsmanship were gone. Miriam had left [indecipherable] firmly behind and was handsome though small. Yeshua and his brothers were all taller than she. There was James[56] who had grown into a broad-shouldered young man clearly meant to follow in his father's trade. Younger[57] than Yeshua were Joses, Judas, and Simon. His sisters[58] Salome and Mary[59] were present as well. Miriam was dressed as one might expect from an Essene, but the daughters were not. This reminded that these were not of her blood. While some thought Joseph an Essene, this was not the case. His children older than Yeshua were not of that sect. Those who were younger, were. However Yeshua, apparently throughout his life, had been simply Yeshua.

Miriam and Salome did not want Yeshua to come east with me. Miriam said, "The important have come to Nazareth to hear him speak. He is singular."[60]

"And the rich have come to hear him as well," Salome said. Miriam scowled at her [step-] daughter, frowning on the interest in wealth. Salome was undaunted and said, "They have brought their daughters. Why would Yeshua leave? You brought tragic sadness with your last visit. The young were murdered, my mother had to flee her home, and even Zacharias, the elderly husband of her cousin Elisabeth, was martyred because he aided in their and your escape. And she

---

56   n.b., this would be his step-brother
57   And these would be half-brothers
58   And finally, these would be, step-sisters older than Yeshua
59   I will translate the sister's name as "Mary" and leave Yeshua's mother as "Miriam." This will make keeping straight the number of women named "Mary" somewhat more manageable.
60   That is to say, unique or special.

was gone soon after. Why should Yeshua follow you now?"

I was saddened to hear this of Zacharias, a pious man, and his wife. "Yeshua would not follow me. We would only travel together," I told her.

Miriam said, "Joseph is old. If Yeshua traveled so far, he would likely never see him again."

"That is no reason to stay," Joseph said softly.

"I would speak for myself," Yeshua said.

"You should, but what you have to say for yourself is of no more weight than what others might say of you," I said. Both Miriam and Salome were still.

Yeshua asked, "Are not my own words, when the subject is mine own self, of more value than the words of others?"

I said, "They are not. Any word spoken of you, whether or not from your own mouth, is only an expression of a perception of you. Be humble and never assume that your own perception of something or someone, even of yourself, has more worth.[61] Words are words, and are equal."

Salome's eyes fixed upon me, and she said, "Use caution, for harm has come to those who anger Yeshua."

Miriam touched Salome's arm and softly said, "Those days are long past."

Yeshua said, "I am humble before my father, but hear my words if they are at least equal. I am a man now. I am free to travel wherever I choose; I am free to lead, follow, and choose company. Mother, what I find here, I can find elsewhere, but what I might find elsewhere, I cannot find here."

Miriam looked downward and I knew then what anxiety there was. Yeshua was considering setting out on the path.

"Come and sit," I said. A circle was formed, and the men

---

61   Paraphrasing the translation here, but I am confident the
      general intent has been conveyed.

and boys sat while the women remained standing. "All sit," I said. The circle was widened and the women sat and filled the new space.

"Tell me of the years since we saw each other last," I said. "What do you mean when you say that important people have sought out Yeshua and that it is a poor choice to anger him."

"I have matured since then," Yeshua said.

Then there was silence until Miriam said, "Learned men have attempted to teach him, but they soon learned that it was Yeshua who was the teacher."

Salome said, "Including one Yeshua struck dead."

I turned to Yeshua. "You killed a man?"

"He has been restored," Yeshua said.

"All whom Yeshua cursed were made whole again," Miriam said quickly. "He healed them all."

"You have the power to curse?" I asked.

"And to heal," Miriam said.

"I would speak for myself," Yeshua said once more and everyone fell silent. "In my youth, I was inconstant. What I can do, I have learned to harness just as one would strap up a beast. Until restrained, in its wildness, it did harm."

"Tell me of the good you have done," I said.

His brother James leaned forward and said, "Once as I collected wood for the fire, and Yeshua was with me, a serpent bit me on the hand. I fell, and felt the poison pass through me. I was at once cold. Death was upon me. Yeshua breathed on my hand. The snake burst into pieces, and I was, in the instant, healed."

Mary, the younger of the sisters, said, "Once, while playing on a roof with other children, another fell and was killed. The parents of the dead child rushed forward and accused

Yeshua of throwing him from the roof. Yeshua stepped from the high roof, landed on his feet, and insisted he had not pushed the dead child, and instead raised him up. The child, named Zenon, once dead, stood and bore witness that Yeshua had not killed him but saved him."

I asked, "The child was raised from the dead?"

"Another child was as well," Joseph said. "A small child, still of an age to nurse, died of disease. Yeshua heard the clamor, ran to the home, and woke the dead child. He then instructed the mother to take the child to her breast. He also told the women to remember him."

"He often did this as a young boy," Miriam said. "He would curse or save someone and then tell them to remember him. Even as young as when you left us, during our passage to Egypt, there were two boys we met along the way. Their names, as I remember, were Dismas and Gestas. They had nothing, no family and were covered in filth, and we caught them as they attempted to steal food. We fed them, and they sat with us, but would not come with us. Yeshua told them to remember him. He promised that someday both would be at his side. We found it very odd. We have not seen those boys since, nor do I expect we ever will."

"I will see them again," Yeshua said. "As will you, mother."

I looked at Yeshua and asked, "Why do you think you were telling these people to remember you? Did you think that raising an infant from death would not be memorable enough?"

"I was very young, but I believe I had some fear of being forgotten," Yeshua said. He paused and then looked directly into my eyes and said, "But you did not forget me."

I said nothing, but I felt a strange pride rush through me. I doubt I could have forgotten Yeshua even if I had never returned to Jerusalem. He was the reason, after all, that I had traveled to the Sindh and learned all that I learned.

After some silence, Joseph rose and said, "Let us go to a home nearby, which I know and once called my own, where my cousins[62] still reside. There we might eat and discuss further Yeshua's coming journey."

And we ate. They ate flesh as did I as we are taught that we should be grateful for all we are given. It was not elephant nor dog nor snake nor the others, and the beast was not killed for me. Still, I mention this because some of the teachings perhaps have me uneasy. As for Miriam and the children of her blood, they were raised in the Essene tradition and rejected the rituals of the Temple, such as animal sacrifice, but they did eat meat. Joseph and the others of course ate clean meat.

Salome said, "Yeshua, come back with us. Do not leave us. Look at the sadness you cause our mother."

Miriam did indeed appear cheerless. Yeshua said nothing, but perhaps was pained. He looked to his mother who did not return his gaze.

"Would you have me be a craftsman, then?" he asked Salome.

"A fine trade. Fine enough for many," Salome said.

"Perhaps not fine enough for me. I was chosen by these travelers from far away," Yeshua said.

Miriam grimaced at this, perhaps not only at the thought of Yeshua departing, but also at the lack of humility in the statement.

I said to him, "You were not chosen. You were recognized. You were not selected as having some unique importance.

---

62 Some sort of relation, perhaps cousins or perhaps surviving relatives of his first wife.

Dawa and the others sought their friend, and in you they found him. This does not speak to your significance or potential. It only means that you continue to be you. They and I hope you will come and resume your learning and teaching. You are promised nothing, not acclaim nor approbation, only the opportunity to work hard and perhaps to grow."

"To what end?" Salome asked. "Why travel and return?"

Yeshua answered before I could. "To grow to understand, to see the light." It was a supposition. He had a way of making a guess sound like a statement of fact. While extremely bright, I know in hindsight that he was merely confidently speculating, a tactic that would prove successful time and again for Yeshua.

"To help others to be set free[63] until all are thus, and then we ourselves may be free from suffering," I said.

"Do you worship in the Temple, Thomas?" Miriam asked.

"I respect all that are wise, and will give my time and ear to anyone," I said.

Miriam asked, "But you do accept the Most High, our Lord?"

"I know of the benevolence present and inside each of us," I said.

Yeshua said, "No matter what I might see or hear in the east, should I accompany you, I will never come to doubt or abandon the one and indivisible God."

I said, "You will be shown reasons to doubt or to abandon nothing but suffering and craving, and even then the decision will still be yours."

"We will go to the Temple tomorrow," Joseph said. "Yeshua must be examined."

While James nodded, Miriam said nothing.

---

63 The text actually reads closer to "all beings to be liberated" but I found it awkward.

"Might I come as well?" I asked.

"We will all go," James said.

So we did. The next day we went to the temple. I did not enter nor did I stand among the women. I stood to one side. Through the door, I could see within. Yeshua stood surrounded by many of the elders, as I had so long ago, and he read. Joseph and James were inside with Yeshua, while Miriam and the others stood watching through a lattice of reeds woven in a screen above the partial wall.

Yeshua read aloud, "Be strong and courageous, fear not, nor be terrified because of them, for Jehovah your God is He who is going with you; He will not fail you nor abandon you."

How appropriate I thought these words were, both for the ritual he was performing and as words of encouragement. I waited to see what Yeshua would decide, and I would have waited much longer. I was in no hurry to return with or without him. Still, the next day, I admit I was surprised when Yeshua decided to return with his family and not accompany me to the east.[64]

Joseph and his family left without formality. I did not know it at the time, but I had seen the last of the old man in this lifetime.[65] I would remember him fondly for his genuine nature and I hope to recognize him again someday.

It occurred to me that I might never see Yeshua again. I did not make immediate arrangements to depart since where one might be is hardly important. It was more important to contemplate all that I had seen and heard.

---

64   *I am truly conflicted here because the text is spare and I am not sure if Thomas was actually surprised or not. In fact, it does not even speak of a decision. In the passage after the reading, in the original text, Yeshua has departed Jerusalem to return with his family.*

65   *Something similar to "lifetime" or "existence"*

On the morning of the second day of my meditation, the Other returned. He had only spoken to me once since I set out on this return journey. The voice, so familiar now, no longer startled me and no longer concerned me. He just was.

"I told you he would not come. This was all in vain. It is time to return to the east. You know Dawa is no longer young. Return to the Sindh. You were fortunate Yeshua chose not to return with you. Why complicate your simple life?"

I said, "As I have told you, I want nothing from you. Doubt would come from craving that which I do not have. I have all that I want and thus, I am without doubt. I will wait until I am done waiting. I will leave when I am ready."

At this he left me and he was not gone an hour when Yeshua returned alone. I smiled at the sight of him.

"You will come with me then?" I asked.

"I will stay in the house where we ate. Come to me tomorrow and we will talk," Yeshua said. To this, I agreed, and we parted.

10

After sunrise, I arrived at the house and was met outside by Miriam, Salome, and James.

"I have come to see Yeshua," I said.

"He is not here," Miriam said.

"Go your way. Leave us alone," said Salome.

Miriam scolded her, and James said, "They have told us he is at the Temple. We are going there now."

"Did he leave your party and return without telling you?" I asked.

James said, "We are not sure he left Jerusalem at all."

When we found him, Yeshua was sitting with ten older men, posing questions and questioning their responses. Miriam held Salome back, and we stood and silently listened.

"Still, could the Lord return a soul to live another life and then another? Is not anything possible for the Father?" Yeshua asked.

"Anything is possible, but is there proof it has happened?" one elder asked in return.

Yeshua said, "Does not the Lord say to Jeremiah, 'Before I formed you in the womb I knew you, before you were born I set you apart.' We must therefore exist before birth."

"This may mean that we are formed and we are with the Most High before we are born, but this is not proof that we have lived before, as man," another elder said.

Yeshua said, "But Solomon wrote, 'Woe be unto you, ungodly men, which have forsaken the law of the most high God! For if you increase, it shall be your destruction; and if you be born, you shall be born to a curse.' Does this not mean a man who has forsaken the law in life might die and be born again, this time to a curse?"

I smiled broadly. He was wise, well-versed, and confident. The men were clearly interested and amused.

His mother finally stepped forward to interrupt. "Yeshua," Miriam said. "You have caused me great anxiety. We have searched for you."

"Why did you search?" Yeshua answered. "Did you not know I must be in the house of the relatives of my father? And did those inside not tell you I would be at the Temple?"

James said, "Do not speak to her in such a way. Her displeasure is a [indecipherable] of her love."

Yeshua replied, "I do not mean to show disrespect. I simply asked questions. How can a query be rude? I was not implying that she has no wit. Just the opposite since I was confused as to why she, with her capacity, would search rather than logically return to the house where we stayed, where she would then be told precisely my whereabouts."

Again, I found myself troubled. How would such an undisciplined[66] youth be able to open himself to the pursuit of enlightenment for himself and others? Even if he was

---

66 *This is perhaps not the best translation, but the wording was somewhat muddled and clumsy. From context, I have surmised this was the author's intent.*

correct in his logic, it was his approach in dealing with others that was disquieting. Clearly, Yeshua could read and he was knowledgeable, especially for a Nazarene,[67] but what good was it to have even the sweetest bread if one would insist on forcing it into the mouths of others? Even those who would gladly listen to him were by him abused. Perhaps it was because Yeshua had rarely met his equal, or because his mother continued to insist on his exceptionality, or perhaps it was due to the ill-treatment that Yeshua surely had taken as the only man-child in Joseph's house who was not of his blood. Not at the hand of kindly Joseph, nor James, but by Nazareth[68] who already feared him for his mystical deeds.

So, he had decided to return with me. Would the teachers, the wise men in the Sindh and beyond, would they be compelling enough to Yeshua that he would listen and learn?[69]

---

67   This reference to Nazareth was not so overt in the text. Instead, it read that Yeshua was knowledgeable for someone who had come from where he had come. It obviously needed my assistance for clarity's sake.

68   Again, an oblique but not actual ref to Nazareth in the original text.

69   Going forward, we now enter into what is sometimes referred to as the "lost years" of Jesus, the years of his adolescence and young adulthood.

II

We set out toward the east in the company of many traders of goods and merchants who spoke in the tongues of the Sindh, the Saka,[70] Pahlavi, and peoples beyond. Yeshua seemed resolved and completely unconcerned. He appeared as if the experiences that lay before him were simply a set of tasks to be accomplished.

We traveled to Damascus. Stopping at a market, we purchased bread. We ate as we talked and walked. Yeshua looked in all directions.

"Are you curious?" I asked.

"When I see that which I have never seen, I admit, I marvel."

"Then, young Yeshua, in the coming times, I promise many marvels indeed," I said.

He did not respond for a moment and then calmly said, "And to you, I say stay steady beside me, and I promise you the same."

---

70 *Interesting this, since save fragments of dialect on some coinage, very little is known of a language of the Saka, separate from Khotanese Saka. It is noteworthy that merchants speaking this little-known language were traveling at least as far as Jerusalem.*

I believed him then, and as I write this, I know it was wise to accept his words as true.

Yeshua looked at the tallest of the structures. I thought him impressed and asked, "Are you awed?"

He never slowed nor hesitated and said, "Some of these[71] will confuse me with a king. I am thoughtful, but not about their great stacks of stones."

"No one will think you a king for your clothes are plain," I said.

"The day will come."

I said nothing. Was this boasting? He had been given to passions, his sister had warned, although Yeshua had claimed he had grown. I ate a bit of bread.

I asked, "How do you know these things?"

"I know what I know," he said softly.

A man of the Sindh called to me and bade me come closer. I did, as we walked, but Yeshua did not. He continued at the same pace, but kept his distance.

"Where are you taking this boy?" the man asked me; his accent was from the sea.[72]

"I am not taking him. We are traveling together."

"What is your destination?" he asked.

"Wherever our path leads," I said.

He paused and then said, "You are one of them."

There were those who refused to seek enlightenment and persecuted those of us who sought to free others and eventually ourselves. This was especially true among those

---

71 *"Some of these" taken to mean "some of these people" as in the residents of Damascus.*

72 *It is likely that this meant the speaker spoke a dialect from the coastal area of his homeland. The word "accent" is close.*

who traveled to the west.[73] I had learned to simply avoid them. They had too far to go. I returned to Yeshua's side, but the man followed.

"Do not travel with him," the man spoke to Yeshua and pointed to me.

"Why should I not?" Yeshua asked.

"The land where we are from is overrun by mindless people who believe that to not have anything is the key to happiness. He will strip you of all you have and you will become as they are—without ambition," he said.

I began to speak, but Yeshua held up his hand and I stayed silent.

Yeshua said, "Has he asked anything of you? Has he taken anything from you?"

The man said, "He has not."

"Then what concern of it is yours?" Yeshua asked.

"You are young and I sought to protect you from a life of poverty and suffering," the man said.

"You are happy?" Yeshua asked.

The man walked along with a beast carrying a great number of goods. His clothing was superior to many in the group of strangers. His face was fleshy, without the points of bones. He had two rings.

"I am happy," the man said.

Yeshua stopped. "You are not. You must travel, away from cousins,[74] and instead of commenting on the air or the fine goods, you try to drive my companion and me apart. A contented man would not do that. You are not coming to my aid. You are selfish and bored and jealous. Had you

---

73   The direction was less clear than I have indicated, but it is more
     than reasonable to assume the direction in question was west.
74   Literally, from the text.

come to us with an open heart, you would have increased the number of your friends. Instead, now you might walk alone, knowing that we are together and we distrust you."

I was surprised at Yeshua's attack on the man. I said, "I harbor no ill will."

We three walked on.

"What would you have me do?" the man asked.

Yeshua said, "Henceforth, judge no one, not even yourself. Let others live as they would and count[75] what you deem important."

The man took a few steps and seemed to consider this, but then he said, "Go worship your Buddha, be happy in your deprivation, and I will continue to think for myself."

I was sad for him, but proud of Yeshua. When the man had made space between him and us, Yeshua asked, "I have heard of Buddha, but you do not worship him, do you?"

"There are far wiser men than I am and who will be your teachers. I can tell you that Buddha is not a god. He is not like your Lord Jehova."

"You no longer believe in the One all-knowing?" Yeshua asked.

"I neither believe nor disbelieve. I know there is an inner light in each of us. I know that Gautama Buddha was a man. I know that I believe we have reached our full potential when we no longer crave and we are released. We seek that which is easeful, not stressful, and everything that has form is stressful but that inner light has no form. We want release from the stressful," I said.

"But is not the wanting of release itself a form of craving? Is not the practice itself an attempt to have that which you

---

75   *Take stock in or reexamine.*

crave?" Yeshua asked.

I smiled at him. "It is, and as a well-known tale from the Buddha shows us that when one reaches the other side of the river, even the raft becomes a burden and must be released."

"But what of…?"

"Yeshua," I said, "please do not ask too much of me. I am merely a student. You will sit with the priests of Brahma and consider what they have to say."

"But you have been a student all this time and you still do not have the answers. Does this mean I will have to wait so many seasons for the answers I seek?" Yeshua asked.

"One thing you will learn, my friend, is patience," I said. I had never referred to him as my friend before and, by his reaction, I doubt many had.

12

I sat with the entire contingent asleep around me and the fire dwindling. The flickering light enchanting[76] me. The Other came to me just then.

"He will bring you to grief. Send him back to his mother."

I replied, "Not once have you been correct with regard to Yeshua. What is it you fear?"

"I fear nothing. You have chosen the wrong path. I am helping you to see."

I asked, "Why do you care if I am on the wrong path?"

"Where you go, I must go."

I whispered, "You may leave me any time you choose. Leave me, and trouble me no more."

"We are joined, we two. We cannot be parted. I can no more be separate from you than you from me."

I whispered, "I do not need you. I do not need these whispers of doubt in my ears. Be gone."

Yeshua rose to one elbow. I thought he was asleep! He asked, "To whom are you speaking?"

He saw no one but me and could not hear the voice. No

one ever had. What would he think?

"To whom are you speaking?" he asked again. His voice was calm.

"I have long had one who comes to me. Speaks to me," I said.

"A spirit?"

"A tempter. The sewer of doubt and fear. I hate him."

"I saw nothing," Yeshua said.

"No one sees or hears him except for me," I said. "He comes for me alone."

"You see him?" Yeshua asked.

"In a fashion, I see him in the corner of my eye. A shadow I cannot look upon directly."

Yeshua considered this and then asked, "Did he come to you when you were a child?"

"When I was a child, he came to me as a child," I said. "I believed then that every person had such a visitor, but I was ridiculed for it. In the village, the people told me that I spoke only to myself."

"And your parents?"

I said nothing.

He then asked, "Is that why they call you Twin? Because there is you and this... tempter?"

"At first, they said it mockingly. I stopped speaking to him aloud and they soon decided it had been but a childish thing, but the name, calling me 'Thomas' persisted," I said.

Yeshua asked, "So you never had a brother?"

I said, "I once had a great many things but now I have nothing. I am working to crave nothing and to find inner peace. It would be easier without the Other."

Yeshua asked, "You cannot keep him away?"

"He says we are bonded," I said.

Yeshua fell silent.

"Please," I said, "tell no one of this."

Yeshua lay down and said, "You have cast your secret down a well, Thomas. I will never speak of it to others."

I smiled. I believed him.

"I would speak with him, with the Other," Yeshua said.

"You cannot hear him," I said. I was afraid.[77]

"You can. You will speak between us. When next he comes to you, I would speak with him, if we are alone," Yeshua said. "We should sleep."

He rolled from me and I sat silently watching the fire once more. It was much diminished. I wondered what Yeshua might say to him. I wondered what he might say in return.

---

77   *We can imagine Thomas's anxiety at such a suggestion. We also wonder at this point if this is a myth, meant to be a supernatural entity, such as the devil or a spirit, or if this is autobiographical, revealing some form of schizophrenia.*

13

After we crossed into the Sindh, in the north, we came through the land of the five rivers[78] and we found ourselves among those Sramana[79] who lived throughout that region. They welcomed us and when the other travelers continued on, we remained. In a particular village lived a man called Padavan who spoke Greek and while he was not a follower of the teachings of Buddha, he was a dedicated student of the jina. Yeshua asked him many questions, as if attempting to draw out all Padavan knew. It was the same, one evening, as we ate.

"So there are three jewels. Right belief, right knowledge, right conduct?" Yeshua asked.

"Yes," Padavan said.

"They live much as the Essene do," I said to Yeshua, who nodded in return. Padavan wore the simplest of cloth, it was white, and he ate no meat. His people could fast for days on end.

"And you must harm no living creature?" Yeshua asked.

Padavan said, "No harm. We brush insects from our path

---

78 *We can assume he means the Panjab here.*
79 *Jainists, more than likely*

lest we step on them. I do not destroy the biting fly on my arm."

"Tell me how jina spread the word," Yeshua said.

Padavan answered, "Jina was branded a heretic for rejecting the rituals and for teaching that salvation was found from within, that only by a man's own effort might he be saved. As a heretic, he could not stay in one place, but instead gathered eleven disciples who followed him and helped him in his teaching. Many others followed as well, but could not commit to total devotion to the way."

"How does one show total commitment?" Yeshua asked.

Without pride Padavan said, "You must live for twelve years as I have. You must do without fine cloth and food, eat the most meager of vegetables and roots, expose your skin to the rain and beating sun."

"And you have completed this?" I asked.

"I have," Padavan said.

"Is there more?" Yeshua asked.

Padavan said, "You will be reborn eight times; you must die and then come back again."

Yeshua fell silent for a moment and then asked, "What is the purpose of your return?"

"To continue to learn, to grow, to improve, until the light within can be the light of the world," Padavan said.

"So, now after your twelve years of hardship are you enlightened or cleansed?" I asked.

Sadness appeared on Padavan's face. "I still contest."[80]

We ate and he ate. A paste of seeds was all he consumed. This he followed with a long drink of hot water. He seemed frail and tired and even resigned. We continued to talk until

---

80   *The particular word here might be said to mean "struggle for control."*

Padavan slowly rose to his feet.

"I apologize, but it is late," he said. His face become grave and he said, "I ask that if I have offended in any way, please forgive." He left us.

"I do not like his aspect," I said.

Yeshua stared in the direction Padavan had gone. "How can he face it?"

I did not understand Yeshua's question until three days hence. We had not seen Padavan. When we came into the light that morning, near the stream, and there on the coarse weeds lay Padavan. He was neither ill nor dead. He simply lay on his side.

"What are you doing?" I asked.

Yeshua asked, "What do you call it?"

"Sallekhana," Padavan said softly.

"What is he doing?" I asked.

"He will die," Yeshua said, not lifting his eyes from Padavan.

"But he is not ill, nor injured," I said.

"I will not eat again. I will not drink again. I will not rise again," Padavan said.

I could not believe it. "Why would you do this to your body?"

"What I do is spiritual. It has little to do with my body," Padavan said.

Yeshua only stared.

I asked, "But what do you hope to gain?"

"I have no certain aim in mind," Padavan said.

This method seemed a poor choice. "Why do you not throw yourself from a mountain top or step into the deep water? Why whither and die in this manner?"

"Living the days is also painful. I do not wish to live longer nor speed the process," Padavan said.

Yeshua said, "Thomas, speak no more."

"We should seek out his people. If not to stop him, then to see him again," I said.

"Enough," Yeshua said.

Padavan said, "I have spoken to them and have consent. I do not want to lie here wistfully thinking of those who went ahead or were left behind. With a calm heart, with peace, I choose. I will meditate and listen as my teacher recites the scriptures and I will be tranquil."

An old man, Padavan's teacher, sat fast by, silently rocking.

"And you believe you will be reborn," I said.

Padavan turned his head, his eyes into mine. He said, "I am not to think about such things. I must think of my 'now,' not steps down the path or lifetimes away."

In all the years I had studied, I had not heard of this practice of the Sramana of simply choosing to lie down in this manner. I had not lived among them, true enough, but Yeshua was even stranger to these people than I and yet had seemed to comprehend quickly. As if even then, even so young, he understood what it was to accept death passively. The people of the village also noticed how sensitive was Yeshua and began to whisper of his great spirit.

On the third day, Padavan was released by his body, and rose to be born again. I wished that he might find enlightenment and peace in his next, but it seemed he might have still had a long way to go.

Yeshua seemed both admiring and disquieted. We had all seen people die, such were the times, but he had never seen a death like Padavan's.

"Such dignity and confidence," Yeshua remarked.

"He accomplished in the manner of his leaving what he could not in the conduct of his stay," I said.

Padavan's teacher took note of Yeshua's wonder and intelligence, and invited Yeshua to become his student. I became concerned at this, since I had not yet returned with Yeshua to where I hoped Dawa awaited our return. Was I to wait all these years, travel all this way, only to lose Yeshua to the Sramana? But in these thoughts, I revealed my weakness and my craving. I would wait to see what Yeshua would decide.

Within days, however, Yeshua had become restless and could no longer stay among them. "We will continue on."

The people of the village begged Yeshua to stay, but we traveled on to Juggernaut.

14

It was in the Mahavana that we came at last to where we would stay for many seasons. Dawa met us there.

Dawa walked with the aid of a rod. I asked, "Have you injured yourself?"

"I prefer three legs to two," he said. He smiled. Truly, I knew I was home. My time here, my years as a student, had been such a period of revelation.

I embraced Dawa and he had aged beyond the seasons. We kissed and then he said, "Yeshua, the priests have been told of your arrival and they would meet you."

"Are they the teachers I was told to expect?" he asked.

"They are this way," Dawa said, pointing down a path with his rod. Yeshua stepped out quickly, attempting to lead although he knew not the way. Dawa and I followed.

"Tell me of him," Dawa said.

I looked ahead at Yeshua who was gaining more and more distance on us. "He is a calm and serious fellow. Curious, and curious."[81] We took him to the place [indecipherable] where he came to the Para-Brahma, the priest called

---

81   *A bit of a translator's fun here.*

Rahula, and the priest called Samiddhi. Dawa spoke first to Samiddhi. "This is one who calls himself Yeshua. He was tested and found to be Gyalwa Nagarjuna, whom we all knew."

Yeshua asked me, "What are they saying?" I told him only to be still.

Rahula asked, "What proof?"

I reached into Yeshua's bag[82] and revealed the cup.

Dawa said, "Our friend wrote of his next coming and a sign in the sky. This we followed and we found the boy of whom we have spoken many times. He selected his cup from among many items. Many seasons have gone, and now Thomas has returned, with the boy turned a man."

"What are they saying?" Yeshua asked again.

"Dawa is introducing you," I said.

Rahula, Samiddhi, and the other white priests came to Yeshua and hands were upon him and kisses.

"Does not even one of them speak Greek?" Yeshua asked.

"Most of us understand you, but there is nothing to be learned here in that tongue. You must learn to read the Vedas," Rahula said. His Greek left much to be desired.

"How will I learn this?" Yeshua said.

"You will have a teacher," Samiddhi said.

I thought back to the stories of young Yeshua and his teachers. "Perhaps I could teach him?" I asked.

Rahula said, "Let him begin with you, and then we shall teach him later."

So his lessons began and Yeshua learned at a remarkable rate to read the scriptures.[83] Soon his pronunciation and interpretation were better than my own, and so Rahula and

---

82   Bag? Bundle?
83   One assumes written in Vedic Sanskrit

Samiddhi took charge of his instruction. I often sat with them.

Samiddhi taught. "On this occasion, the Buddha was teaching and his devoted follower, one held in great favor called Sariputta, found himself on the wrong side of the river. It appeared swift and deep. There was no ferry, nor was there a bridge. Sariputta said, 'I will not be dissuaded. I will hear the teaching of the Blessed One,' and he stepped out onto the surface of the water and it was firm beneath his foot. The water was swift, but was not deep. The granite was close beneath the surface; the colors and water fooled the eye. This was only discovered because Sariputta had the faith and will to step forward. He walked across. Near the middle, the river deepened, and his courage waivered for a moment, but fortifying himself, he continued to the far bank and then came to the Blessed One and heard the teaching. The people were surprised to see him and to him said, 'How did you come?' Sariputta said, 'I lived unaware until I heard the voice of the Blessed One. As I was desirous to hear of the escape from suffering, I walked over the swift waters because I had faith. Faith enabled me to do so, and now I am here in the bliss of the Buddha's presence.' The Buddha, the most exalted one, said, 'Well said, Sariputta. This sort of faith can save the world from craving and their differences and their envy and enable to walk across to bliss. You all must always move forward, across the gulf, to end bitterness and to cross the river of worldliness and attain deliverance from death.'"

"He did not, in truth, walk upon the water," Yeshua said.

"He crossed by means of faith," Samiddhi said.

"Still, he led the people to believe he walked upon the river," Yeshua said.

"Do not miss the point for concern of the details,"

Samiddhi said. "We do not even know if any of this occurred. The story is not about Sariputta. The story is about faith as an enabling force."[84]

Yeshua said, "Odd that it would seem acceptable to you to use a story built around a falsehood to teach the value of faith."

Samiddhi only smiled. As for myself, I did not. The Other, however, laughed.

Yeshua pushed them every day until both priests were exhausted with his questions and his interpretations. Dawa and Samiddhi told Yeshua there was no need of haste. To learn something in months or to learn it in days, in either case you have only learned it. Dawa told him there was no advantage to learning it quickly; after all there was no limit.

Yeshua said he understood. "I do not crave to be first, or to boast. I only hope to gather the knowledge as a farmer gathers a crop. Why would someone slow the farmer in his progress?"

*   *   *

Seasons passed and I taught Yeshua other knowledge that I had learned here, such as the working of wood. We made plows and yokes. We crafted oars for boats, and we worked

---

84   *This is reasonably close. I feel I've captured the essence of what Samiddhi is attempting to say. I must admit becoming quite drained at times from the effort of trying to distill some sort of concise and cogent point from some of these passages. I am humbled at the opportunity to do work of such import while, at the same time, relieved that it was I, with my particular rarified skills and knowledge, who came upon the manuscript. Honestly, I am sad to admit, I have even known several of my colleagues who could not have managed such a task under such conditions and time constraints.*

on a small boat.

I said to him, "See how much easier it is to shape wood rather than stone."

Yeshua said, "That which is quicker to shape is quicker to ruin."

*   *   *

And there came a day when I watched as he sat with Samiddhi. I could not hear their words, but I watched as Samiddhi taught Yeshua. The Other came to me then and said, "Yeshua has supplanted you here. He impresses them, as you never did. Even Dawa prefers him."

"And I am proud of Yeshua and happy for him," I said.

"Go and listen, so that Samiddhi will not teach Yeshua that which he has hidden from you."

"Be gone," I said. Samiddhi had always been kind and generous, and I knew the Other wanted to defame him, to once again create doubt. As I approached Yeshua and Samiddhi, they stood. We three went to the limit of the village. There an old man sat by the water's edge, unable to see. I did not recognize him as he was from another place.

Samiddhi took his hand. "Look with care at his eyes," Samiddhi said. Yeshua and I looked. The eyes were caked with filth. They were covered as if by a mortar the color of desert sand. I had seen this before.

"Why have you not washed your eyes?" Yeshua asked.

"When I wash them," the old man said, "that which is hard becomes soft and thick, the more water I add the worse it is for me, and it comes into my eyes. Now if I pull them open, I will tear the eyes from my face. If I wet them, it only spreads. My eyes are ruined."

"Is there nothing we can do?" Yeshua asked.

"It is time I teach you this," Samiddhi said. He reached down into the soil near his feet. From the soil in his hand, he removed a small stone and cast it away. He withdrew from his purse[85] a small jar. This he opened and sipped from it and then dribbled into his hand. He handed the jar to me. It smelled sweet. I knew it to be a mixture of honey[86] and oil. We watched as Samiddhi worked the liquid and soil together in the palm of his hand into a paste. This he began to gently rub onto the man's eyes. At first, only to cover but then, as he rubbed, the soil and the illness mixed together. The man cried out.

"Do not open your eyes. Do not attempt it," Samiddhi told him. Yeshua got so close to the man that I thought he might kiss him.

"Will this heal him?" Yeshua asked.

"Perhaps not in the first attempt. Perhaps not at all if there is yet another sickness beneath," Samiddhi said.

"Wash your eyes," I told the man.

"But the water makes them worse, I told you," the man said.

"Wash your eyes. You must have faith," Samiddhi said.

The man stepped into the water and went to his knees. He lowered his face. He washed his eyes. The sickness came away with the soil Samiddhi had placed there. The man opened his eyes and cried out in pain.

"Wash your eyes, continue," Samiddhi said.

The man placed his face in the water and rubbed them beneath the surface. He raised his face, his eyes nearly closed, swollen and red. He walked to us. I looked into

---

85 *It seems to be the best word, but perhaps a small sack.*
86 *I am unsure if "honey" is the best translation here.*

his eyes, which now were open. They were red and much abused, but the sickness was gone. He could see.

"This an act of God," Yeshua whispered to me.

"It is an act of faith and knowledge," I answered.

"What shall I do?" the man asked Samiddhi.

"Wash your eyes, again and again, in clean water. Stay far from waste and decay. Some days from now, if your eyes are better, go about your life. If the sickness begins to return, seek me out," Samiddhi said.

"My eyes will be clean," the old man said and he was gone. I never saw him again.

Yeshua asked, "How did the addition of soil cleanse?"

Samiddhi said, "Like is with like. The sickness that would not be washed away would mix with the soil, and the soil would be washed away with water. Sometimes the way to remove the unwanted is to dilute the impurity[87] and thereby weaken it."

"And so why have you not cured this land of all blindness?" Yeshua asked. "I have seen the sightless begging in the neighboring villages."

"There are many types of blindness," I said. "There are those for whom sight can be restored and then there are those whose present path is destined to be unlit."

Yeshua paused and looked from Samiddhi to me and back. He said, "I would find a way to restore the sight of all."

"We all have a path to follow. We each have our own lessons to learn. While it may always seem preferable to ease the suffering of others, it is also true that sometimes people have a certain lot in life," Samiddhi said.

"Who determines such a thing? Why would our Father

---

87   *A bit cheeky, I know, but I have conveyed the spirit of what was in the text.*

give us the power to ease the suffering of one who is undeserving? It would seem the arrival of a means of deliverance is at once the proof that such a deliverance is deserved," Yeshua asked.

"Temptation does not make one worthy," a voice from behind said. It was Rahula. "A man born blind is meant to be blind. It is in the trial that he will learn that which he needs." He stepped into our circle. Samiddhi lowered his head. Not in reverence or even in some sort of accepting deference, but in acquiescence.

Yeshua asked, "But how do you determine who is worthy of aid and peace?"

Rahula said, "We do not have to. This has been predetermined. We have discussed this many times, Yeshua."

Yeshua said, "Not predetermined by God."

"There is no God as you understand it," Rahula said.

"As I have always told you, never will my faith be shaken in my Father," Yeshua said. "No matter what I learn here."

"The people are divided. You have been among the Brahmana these years, and have been among the others, and have read our scriptures. We are for whom the Vedas [indecipherable] and the Kshatriyas, but the Vaisyas may only listen to the readings of the Vedas on the feast days, and the Shudras may not even gaze upon the Vedas, nor hear the readings," Rahula said. "The Shudras are trapped in a world of suffering. They crave much and they may hope to move toward growth and enlightenment in the next, but for these days, their fates are sealed."[88]

---

88 Disclosure—the text here is really a hodgepodge of ideas and is disjointed. It is only with my understanding of 1st century belief systems in the region that I am able to add a modicum of clarity to the passage thus far and to the remainder of the ms to

"But the Vedas would give hope to the Shudras," Yeshua said. I hung my head. This was a tired debate between them.

"Death alone can free them from servitude," said Rahula. "Leave them to their fates, or the [indecipherable] will be angry with you."

"God, my Father, does not count his children differently, all are equally dear to him. The Shudras are as dear to him as the Brahmana," Yeshua said.

"Yeshua, enough. You are being impolite," I said. He had taken the debate too far this time. Yeshua seemed surprised at my words and fell silent. Rahula was also silent and as he stepped away, he looked back at Yeshua once.

"Why do you provoke Rahula thus?" Samiddhi asked. "Is this pride? Has he shown you anything but kindness and generosity?"

"I did not boast, I only spoke the truth," Yeshua said.

"Your truth, but this is not your place," Samiddhi said. He looked toward the retreating Rahula. "This is not a man to make an enemy."

"Perhaps he will understand it was the hubris of youth," I said.

Yeshua turned to me at this and, as our eyes met, I felt foolish.

come.

15

There was a woman. She was from the sea and had come to this place with her family as a child. She knew of the Father and of the path, but had not given her heart to either. She was older than Yeshua and younger than I and she was fierce. She plaited the hair of women but many came to hear her speak as much as to have her work their hair. She was from Magdala, from the shore in our homeland, and she could speak in the local tongues and the tongue[89] and Greek. There were others, too, spread throughout this land who had come from the mountains and worshipped idols, and even as far as Egypt and kept the Sabbath, but Yeshua showed little difference.

This woman was different and was also known as Mary, just as Yeshua's sister was. We called her Magda.[90] There were women in the Mahavana, exotic and mysterious, and a great many came with interest to Yeshua, but Yeshua was drawn to Magda.

---

89 *Aramaic? Hebrew?*
90 *At the very least, it is how I will differentiate between the women named Mary. There are yet even more in subsequent chapters. It was an extremely popular name at the time.*

"I know you and from where you have come," Yeshua told her.

"You may know from where I have come, but you do not know me," she said.

The women present laughed at this. Yeshua did not become angry or shamed.

"You plait hair and wild stories for these women," Yeshua said.

"I plait their hair for the men, I plait the stories because the men are dull," she said.

Yeshua smiled at this. I had never seen him smile this way before. She continued to work.

"Tell my story, someday," Yeshua said.

"You are also dull," Magda said.

Yeshua's smile remained. "I will try to be less so."

16

Yeshua walked among them. The Shudras sat all around, a large gathering, perhaps two dozen. Magda sat among them. They looked up at him with expectant faces as he spoke. I would see this again. Throughout his life, crowds would gather and sit and listen.

"He is among them once more," the Other said.

"He has done this for more than a year.[91] He understands the risk," I said.

"He does this in defiance of the Brahmana," the Other said. "He does it because he is certain of his righteousness. He does it because he feels he is superior. He fully understands the risk to you and he does not care. He does it to impress her."

"I understand his pity. Even Buddha spoke against the caste system[92] and the use of the Vedas in this way," I said.

Yeshua held his arms outstretched and said, "It is what you hold in your hearts, your thoughts and deeds, which will make you noble."

"See how he sounds in his teachings," I said. "In our time,

91 *A number of seasons at least; estimate perhaps 12-18 months.*
92 *My translation here, much simplified.*

he has come amongst these people as Buddha did and as he would again."

"You know this cannot end well for him, nor for her," the Other said, and was gone. I watched Yeshua continue to hold the crowd. Of course he could not choose an easy way for himself; there was only one way. There would be no dissuading him. I had no idea what path lay before us then, but even if I could have foretold all, I doubt it would have made any difference to Yeshua. He was possessed of great purpose. Still, there would be so many regrets for the woman.

"All are equal in the eyes of the Father. Your greatness comes from within, not from without. None are inferior, none are superior, all are equal," Yeshua said. I shook my head and stared. Just this, just saying these words was enough to fall foul of powerful men, and while no one had moved against him, the day would come.

"There is light within each of you. You need not wait for the next life. Ease the suffering of your neighbor who suffers. Do not covet the neighbor who does not. As the Enlightened One said, you must not crave for craving is the root of all suffering," Yeshua said.

"Do not pray to stones. Do not ask idols for forgiveness. They cannot hear. Look to yourself and to your Father who placed his light in each of you. Have no secret desire. Let loose your secrets. His word is clear and it is not in the Vedas, which come not from the Father. Help one another; guard the weak and sick, look to what you might give instead of what you might take. Blessed are those who labor by the sweat of their bodies, for they shall sooner see the light than the idler," Yeshua said.

Magda seemed to sense what Yeshua would say next, just

as I did. She rose as I walked forward. Yeshua glanced at each of us.

He said, "The Brahmana and the Kshatriyas, their priests and those who would humiliate those who sweat and bleed as they sit and feast, they will learn that they are the Shudras of the spirit and you will all see that you, all of you, are the truly rich; all of you are sons and daughters of God."

I stopped but Magda went to him, placed her hand on his chest, and whispered to him. As I watched her touch him, I must admit that I wanted.

17

In the next seasons, when hunger gripped the land, the Shudras asked Yeshua for prayers that would feed them and their children. Yeshua told them that there were no words that could feed them.

"Words are only words, they are only sounds. These sounds can help you to find peace. These words can help you to accept your difficulties and you might sooth the pain of others. Still, these words cannot feed you," Yeshua said.

"But there is no food. We have not the land to grow what we need and the water is here. We will all perish," said a man.

"We are surrounded, in every direction, with fields which could feed all," Yeshua said. He extended his hand toward a large field of rice, ready for the harvest.

"But this is a field of the Brahmana. We may work it, but not eat," the man said.

"The earth and the water and the stalk and the grain are given to us by the Father. You have labored in the fields, and so you have made payment by the sweat of your bodies. You scattered the seed and if you did not work the harvest, the grain would stay where it is," Yeshua said. "As things are, you and your children will starve."

"What would you have us do?" a woman asked. She seemed worn, as if exhausted by decades of toil.[93] "Would you have us take what was not given us?"

To take what is not given is expressly forbidden. One should not take even that which is clearly abandoned if it was not given to you.

"Do not take what is not given to you," Yeshua said to them.

"Then how?" a man asked. The crowd became restless.

"A man once wondered what had given him all of his days, and so he set out to find the source, and he lost many seasons searching for it," Yeshua said. He held both hands high. "Do not take what is not given to you, but do not give what is yours."

"But we have nothing!"

"You have what your Father has given you. You have what you have always given. Your work and effort. If they would not share the rice of the field with you, do not harvest it for them," Yeshua said.

A silence fell over the crowd. There was a realization. I was made sick. What had he done?

"You will all be killed," the Other hissed loudly in my head. I slapped him away.

The crowd erupted into a cheer. It was as if a great fire had been lit. They rushed Yeshua. I saw Magda thrown to the ground. I forced my way into the bodies; the voices were loud. I called to her, but could not find her. Waving arms struck my face and head. I was pushed on all sides. I saw above the crowd on a large stone sat Yeshua and Magda, safe. The people moved around them, arms lifted, voices calling. I

---

93   Character development mine.

saw them on the stone as the crowd pressed on me. Magda was smiling, looking at Yeshua. Yeshua did not look at her. His eyes locked with mine. He was calm, and the look of him quieted me. I became passive and floated in the current of bodies. They began chanting.

"Yeshua. Yeshua. Yeshua. Yeshua."[94]

---

94   *We can assume that this is what they were chanting, although the text was silent on this point.*

18

Dawa came to me and told me that the Brahmana and the Kshatriyas, the priests and the warriors, were coming to Yeshua.

"They mean to see if it was truly he who set the Shudras to their idleness," Dawa said.

"It was he, as you know," I said. "What is their intent?"

"They mean only to question him," Dawa said.

"But you know it will not end with this," I said.

Dawa paused and then said, "What he does, it creates craving in the Shudras. He is creating suffering for those who had none."

"Those who are hungry might not crave if they might keep a mind of love, but it is difficult to do so when it is not only your own hunger, but the hunger of your children," I said. "There is the issue of fairness."

"There is no fairness. That is a word born of competition and envy and craving," Dawa said softly.

I said, "That is simple for the victor to say." I love Dawa still as I write this; it gave me no joy to speak to him thus.

Dawa walked off some distance and Rahula and other white priests arrived with those of the Kshatriyas among them. I followed Rahula to Yeshua, who did not stand and waited to raise his eyes.

"Have you seeded unhappiness among these people?"

"Are not you and the priests more responsible for that than I?" Yeshua asked.

"We have shown you nothing but love and taught you our language and shared the truth with you and you have caused such strife and brought discontent," Rahula said.

"What did you expect in return for your love and truth?" Yeshua asked. "Were these not given freely?"

Rahula said, "What do you hope to gain?"

"What do you hope to withhold for yourselves? I grant them nothing my Father has not already granted us all, for we are all equal in the eyes of God," Yeshua said.

"With your words, you have granted them power they should not have, should not want, and you have caused them to desire that which they cannot[95] have," Rahula said.

"What have I done except revealed to them that all of the Father's children are of great worth?" Yeshua asked.

In the distance, the Shudras sat watching. I did not know if they could hear or not, but they watched.

"Look at them," Rahula said. "What do you see? And now look at me once more. What do you see? Do you see equals? Do you not see the difference? What do you see when you look at them and look at us?"

"I see the Buddha," Yeshua said. "What is it you see?"

At this, Rahula said nothing and departed. I shook my head. This was clever, since what you see in others is a reflection of your own heart, but perhaps not wise. Yeshua was making it impossible for coexistence with the likes

---

95   *This was either "cannot" or "should not"*

of Rahula. Dawa did not depart with them, nor did he approach me. He looked saddened and then he walked to the Shudras and spoke to them.

"Yeshua," I said. He turned to face me. "Even when what you say is true, it may not be prudent."

"I will say what I will say," Yeshua said. "I would have these people know that they are also the Father's children."

He turned and walked to the Shudras. When he arrived, Dawa turned to face him. The expression on Dawa's face softened and then changed into a gentle smile. He stepped to Yeshua and embraced him.

In the days that followed, the Brahmana agreed to share the harvest if the Shudras would bring it in. The share was small but it was a share, after all. I admit I had such joy![96] I knew it could not be the same again. Yeshua had changed the land. As I write this, my feelings on that day seem prideful now.

*   *   *

Within four nights, Dawa came to us. "They mean to kill Yeshua."

"Kill him? Surely the Brahmana would not do such a thing to him over the issue of the rice," I said.

"The issue was never the rice," Yeshua said.

Dawa said, "If not kill him, they may brand him."

"Brand him? He has not taken a life, nor lain with family, nor drank wine, nor stolen the metal.[97] Why not simply banish him?" I asked.

---

96 *Here was, in fact, one of the few expressions of emotion the narrator shares, although he didn't literally use the word for "joy."*

97 *Presumably gold.*

"They fear he will spread his discontent and there are those that would spare his life but brand him to mark him notorious.[98] Others still thought to remove his tongue," Dawa said.

Shudra men came also and spoke of impending danger for Yeshua. One among them said, "The servants of the Brahmana have been sent to kill you."

Dawa spoke to Yeshua. "You must leave this place. You must seek a new place and a new peace. Go out into the world unmarked and perhaps more cautious."

So in the dark, Yeshua and I resolved to depart and we went to Magda. She resisted and Yeshua said to her, "I wish it," and kissed her on the mouth and she continued.[99] Yeshua said, "If she will not leave, I cannot."

The Other whispered, "I warned you. He will get her killed. He will bring to all[100] of us."

I lowered my head and stepped away. I felt Yeshua's hand on my back and I turned.

"He is talking to you now," Yeshua said.

"He says that you will get all of us killed," I said.

"Tell him I command him to leave you," Yeshua said.

"He is laughing at you," I said.

"I will drive him out," Yeshua said.

"I will kill him," the Other said.

"I am trapped," I said to no one.

Magda came closer to us. "What is it?"

Yeshua turned to her. "Come with us. Not because you feel you must, but simply because you want to. Do not follow. Lead if you must. We will not leave without you."

---

98 *Perhaps "tarnished" would be a better fit?*
99 *To resist, one assumes, but perhaps to kiss?*
100 *Perhaps "...bring [death] to all...."*

Magda stepped to me. She looked into my eyes and I felt as if she saw too much.[101]

"Strangle her!" the Other hissed.

I wanted her to come with us. She was beautiful.

She stepped back. She turned to Yeshua. "I will go with you."

We embraced Dawa and [indecipherable] we left and journeyed to the child-place of the Buddha himself.

---

101 *Flourish mine.*

19

We climbed into the mountains and came to Kapilavastu where Gautama Buddha had been a child. It was here that Yeshua perfected his use of Pali and once again spoke to the lowest of the people and they adored him. There were few enemies and there was time for love to grow.

I also could not suppress my craving, and as much as Magda's fondness for Yeshua had grown, he neglected her in favor of his studies. It was then that I, too, grew to love her. I worked every day to weaken my want of her but I could not help myself. I did not crave gold and I did not crave for all the people to know me as they knew Yeshua. I did not crave to be heard and I did not even crave wisdom. I lived my life as well as I could, but I could feel my weakness when the woman was near. She was mesmerizing and mysterious, and yet seemed to remain simple and true. She was not like a whispered secret but more a natural one. When I woke in the mornings, I thought to see her, and then when I did, it was both warm and painful. Thus was the suffering born of craving.

Yeshua, for his part, hardly spoke to her for those seasons, so deeply was he lost to learning. Word of Yeshua's deeds and teachings had spread and the priests of the region refused him the Vedas, but the Shudras had their own secret scrolls and in these Yeshua immersed himself.

Magda and I spoke at length into the night about the path. She was a quick mind, powerful with rhetoric, but open to truths and to my heart's words. On one occasion, I weakened. She stood close by, and while she spoke, I reached out my hand to her face. She fell silent and I thought that my hand would feel her skin, when at the final moment, she withdrew. Her eyes did not look angry. They seemed filled with sympathy. I pulled back my hand.

"Forgive me," I said.

"What you do, you do on behalf of your heart. I have known your heart for some time. I see how you look at me. More, I have seen how you look away from me. There is no shame in how you feel, but if you believe that craving what you can never have is the source of all suffering, then you have chosen a path of pain," Magda said.

"I have not chosen it as much as it has chosen me," I said.

She smiled sadly. "Abandon this. I do not want to be the source of your suffering."

I said, "I work to change these thoughts and feelings. I will work more. You know my desire now; perhaps that alone will help. Love without hope often dies of its own accord."

She turned and walked away. I saw her go. I wanted to attain that level where I would no longer hope.

"You have lost something precious," The Other whispered.

I nodded. "But it was not the woman."

If Yeshua knew of any of this at the time, he said nothing.

*   *   *

We spent many seasons there. I grew to find a way, if not to suppress my cravings, to at least hold my tongue. What had been a stabbing pain changed into a dull ache of desire whenever I was with Magda. I did my best to act the friend and not to betray my true feelings. Not only to rid myself of suffering and to protect Magda from feelings of sympathy but also because of my loyalty[102] to Yeshua.

The people of Kapilavastu and the surrounding [indecipherable] loved Yeshua and they came to listen. He taught and the people marveled at how expert he was with the language and in explaining the sacred texts. My knowledge of Pali was not as good, but Magda did not know the tongue, so I translated as best I could when Yeshua spoke.[103]

"Do not lie," Yeshua said. "Do not spend your lives doing that work which you find meaningless or distasteful. Eventually, the truth will be revealed. With time, every secret is exposed. Especially the secrets you keep from yourselves. Especially the lies you tell yourselves."

She gripped my hand.

"If you heed my words, your lives will fill with happiness. Every stone will clear from your path. However, if you hold fast to your secrets and do work you despise, you will only breed envy and turmoil in your hearts. When you hate the work he gives you, it is not possible to make the master happy. Love the task and you will love the master," Yeshua said.

---

102 *Perhaps not an exact translation, but the actual word was unknown to me (and thus unknown to everyone, I am quite certain) and so I inferred thus, and the subsequent preposition, from context.*

103 *Oh, the load placed upon us polyglots. What follows, it is not lost on me, is the translation of the words of Yeshua by Thomas, and then those are translated, in turn, by me.*

I will admit it was made more difficult by my having to speak of love to Magda in the translation. Yeshua watched us as we sat and as I translated his words. I felt as a thief must, peering into windows, assaying reward and weighing risk. Yeshua, always perceptive, must have seen also and he sent me away.

He came to me soon after and said, "Thomas, we have been in the mountains too long. We will return to Jerusalem. You will go ahead. Seek out my cousin[104] John and my brother James. Do not tell anyone but James that I am returning."

"But your mother?" I asked. "I should not seek her out? Even then, will not James tell her?"

"Tell no one but James that I return," Yeshua said. "Tell James I wish no one to know."

I did not want to go. I did not want to be so far from Magda. I said, "Should Magda journey with me?" I immediately felt foolish. Yeshua only stared at me. The shame![105] Magda walked away without a word.

"But I have become a man of this place; I am not of our old homeland any longer. I have found the path," I said.

"Thomas, because you stray from the path, you must take another. Go, I will follow. We will spread the teachings of the Most Holy Buddha and the Holy Father and we will free many from suffering," Yeshua said.

The Other said, "You need not obey him."

I realized then that I would either serve Yeshua or The Other. "He is the master now," I said. I watched as Magda entered the dwelling.

"I am your friend," Yeshua said. He put his hand upon my brow.

---

104 Cousin or relative.
105 He must have felt shame, in addition to feeling foolish.

"I will go wherever you wilt," I said. I prepared to journey once more to Galilee.

III

We can easily forgive a child his fear of the dark;
real tragedy is men who are afraid of the light.
—Plato

Translator's Notes

What follows is the period commonly known as the ministry of Jesus of Nazareth. There are many similarities with the gospels and there are differences and omissions. What would be of interest would be a comparative study between this treatment of the ministry of Jesus and others, as my discovery would surely become the touchstone document, more important than the hypothetical Quelle text perhaps.

It is my thought that such a work, in addition to this manuscript, would actually merit publication without, as so many colleagues have done, hiring some obscure press in Nebraska to print copies so that they might load them into the trunk of their cars and pass them out at family reunions.

I understand that this manuscript might prove to be controversial because it appears that many of the miracles ascribed to Jesus are herein apparently explained as less than supernatural. It is, of course, up to the reader to decide what he or she believes. This is not an attack upon Christianity; I am merely the humble translator and transcriber.

Your quarrel, in short, would not be with me, but instead

with Thomas himself, as this continues to be a faithful translation of his account.

20

I traveled alone, with The Other. I made my way through villages. Those I met asked of me, and I said I was traveling west[106] to prepare the path of my master. Once, I met a small group of men and one woman.

"But who is your master? And why would he send his servant out with so little?"

"He is one who teaches that we are perfect and that we must all love our brothers and sisters and be kind to all," I said.

"What gods has he that he believes all are perfect?"

I said, "No gods like you, fashioned with your hands of stone or clay. No gods such as you have, that scurry about on four legs. He knows the Father has put wisdom and intelligence[107] and the light in each of you so that you might find the path to contentment and enlightenment."

The Other said, "Good. Good. Continue to speak. See how you cause consternation among their priests. When Yeshua comes this way, they may kill him, and then you may have the woman."

"I have no such motives!" I whispered.

---

106 Simplifying here.
107 Perhaps "intellect" is a better fit here, or even "curiosity."

They wondered. One man asked, "You do not want contentment? You do not want enlightenment?"

"I want contentment. I want freedom from my cravings," I said.

"Once you have all that you want, you will crave no more?"

The Other said, "Once you have the woman, you will crave no more."

I said, "Once a man attains all he craves, he will crave those things he did not know he wanted. You must train yourself to not crave, since craving is the root of all suffering."

"Your master taught this? This sounds like the words of the followers of Gautama, and we have heard this before."

The Other said, "Yes, your master taught this, and then he craved and took the woman." Truly, the Other had not spoken so often since I was a child as he had since Magda had come into my life.

"Enough, be still," I said.

"We will not," the group said. "We know who you are now."

I said to them, "He who sent me speaks it in a different way. He teaches that we all have value, given to us by an all-powerful and unseen Father, with a light in our hearts."

The people revealed many idols, of gods and god-animals. They said, "The gods are not unseen."

"These were made by the hands of those who cannot see god," I said.

"These gods are powerful."

"God does not share his power with stones nor with animals. With man alone did he share his breath."[108]

---

108 *This is the literal translation. I leave it as it is, since the context makes it somewhat obvious that the point is that God has breathed some divinity into man, I felt strangely lyrical and thought it best to leave it as is.*

"You will incur the wrath of our gods."

"If your idols are powerful, may they strike me dead now," I said. "In this instant."

The people were afraid.

"Do not say such things," The Other said. "The risk is not to you alone!"

When the people fell silent, I said, "Know this. If you want peace, be kind to one another. That which you can divide, divide it and share. Do not see in yourself the center of the whole world, and do not make your neighbor to lay humbly."

The Other asked, "And do not covet what others have?"

I thought of Magda. I looked at the people who listened, they marveled at my words, although their priests whispered. There was a sigh in my heart, but with sudden tears, I said, "And do not covet what others have." Perhaps I could free myself of Magda after all.

The Other laughed. "It is not that simple. I see it still, buried within you. She still grips at your [indecipherable]."

The people began to talk amongst themselves, repeating my words. The priests were clearly angry. I departed.

The Other asked, "Did you spread his teaching, or did you seed his death, since you know that Yeshua must come through this valley and those priests will still be there?"

"What I did, I did with peace. I did nothing to harm another. The people worshiped stones they had shaped; they worshiped at the feet of goats. They begged animals and idols for release and for the answers that each man and each woman carry within. Truly, this cannot lead to harm. I began to heal myself, because I shared pure words. The only poison was you," I said.

After that, I did not hear The Other's voice again until I reached the spring at Bethany.

21

I searched for John and was directed east of the Jordan. When I came to the springhead, only a short walk from the river, I found him clothed in rough cloth lashed round with hide.

While I had wondered about my own soundness, I knew listening to this man that he was not at peace. He shouted nearly every word he spoke. He ate the insects, figs, and the stickiness of the trees.[109] He sat at the edge of the spring with his feet in the waters, which ran clear, unlike the mud-filled river.

"Your cousin comes, he has spent these years becoming a learned and a great teacher. I prepare the way," I said.

"Then I shall prepare the way!" he said.

"He is mad," said The Other.

"I know," I said.

"I know! I know I shall prepare his way!" John said.

John stood. He lifted a branch of wood. The Other wanted to leave.

John looked at the men who sat and lay about nearby.

---

109 n.b. "wild honey" from the synoptic gospels appears to be tree sap.

There were only nine of them. All men, all filthy. John called to them. "There is one who is coming! He is coming! Repent!" None of the men moved. One looked up from a rock, and then rested his head once more.

"Awake! For I am the voice in the wilderness that Isaiah foretold!" John said. More people, previously unseen, came from the shrubs and trees. These seemed more amazed than the nearby men. They came close.

"Come! Let me wet you, so that you might be altered!"

A woman stepped into the water and John wet his hand at wiped it across her brow. "Go in peace!" he said. "Freshly born and renewed!"

The Other said again, "He is mad."

"John, we would speak with you," I said.

He stopped. "We?"

I had not realized my words, but pushed on. "I learned long ago of your losses, of your parents."

"Dead! A father I never knew but from stories, a mother not much more than a shadow in my eye."

The kind Zacharias and Elisabeth had helped me and gave me hope when both were scarce and times were dire.

"In halves! They stabbed my father and then sawed him in halves for not revealing how Yeshua and I might be found!" John said.

"Mad," The Other said.

John said, "And my mother's heart never healed of it. She lay down and died some days later."

"So how did you live?" I asked.

"As a boy, I lived here! I lived here and the Lord God gave me to eat and drink and clothe myself! I lived through God's mercy!" he said.

His skin was dark and his hair was in knots. His hands had

known nothing soft. As he baptized more of the people who approached, I left. I went to find James, Yeshua's brother. I went to the Galilee.

22

When I found James, he was a shaper of stones as his father had been. The method and tools had changed little. He was skilled, but still I could see that the people of this region could not see the Buddha in the stone. I thought back to another time, and I longed to see my old teacher, Menelaus, once more, but surely he too was dead by now. I wondered about Dawa. In any event, I was not here for such things. Yeshua would return to this land and I knew that nothing would be as it had been.

I told James that Yeshua was returning, that within days he might be among us. James, as I had thought, wanted to tell his mother, his brothers, his sisters. He spoke of Joseph's death, of an old man who stopped breathing in his sleep. Then, I told him of Yeshua's instruction to not tell Miriam.

"Always of a different sort. Always the designer of events," James said.

"Do you think we should defy him and tell your mother?" I asked.

James turned from me and retrieved another stone. "We will do as Yeshua tells us."

*   *   *

On the eleventh day after my arrival, I had eaten and slept with James those days and nights, Yeshua arrived with Magda, and a beast. She rode atop the animal, with possessions.

I feared her arrival and welcomed it. There was something different in me. I felt more able to resist now. Just the time and distance to find my center[110] had certainly helped. Yeshua and James embraced warmly, and there was laughter. Magda smiled at them, and then at me, and Yeshua brought her to James and he kissed her. Then we went into the house and ate bread with herbs and oil.

"What will you do? You may join me and we might build together," James said.

"I have come to build in a different way," Yeshua said.[111]

"We have come to teach," Magda said. They were partners, even in the teaching.

"A woman who teaches men?" James asked.

"The Father has made us all, and our hearts are the same. There is much to learn from women," Yeshua said.

"And yet, you hide from your mother and sisters?" James asked.

"What I must do, I must do without my former self and there is too much of that in them," Yeshua said. "I am sent by the Father to help these people find the new light within them, the suppressed light."[112]

---

110 *This is the sentiment, if not the exact words.*
111 *Or perhaps "build a different way."*
112 *In actuality, the literal language was quite muddled; I barely managed to cobble together the gist of this scene from the text.*

*   *   *

Yeshua, James, Magda, and I went to see John. We journeyed to the river and then across it and on the third day we arrived. On this day, there were many people. A great crowd stood all around, and John was baptizing. Among them were the Pharisees and Sadducees, standing aside. John saw them, but he did not see us.

To the Pharisees, John said, "Snakes! Repent! You are not chosen among the people! You cannot point to Abraham as your ancestor and think that you are special! God can make the dull stones into the children of Abraham if he so chooses! Any tree that does not bear fruit may be chopped down and burned! Bear fruit and be repentant! All of you! Share with those who have nothing. Do not cling to your possessions. Share your garments and your food! Take only what is fair, what is your right. Do no harm and do not threaten!"

James looked at me. He said, "He is as mad as you said."

Yeshua asked, "You have not seen him before now?"

James said, "I have only heard stories of our cousin in the wilderness."

The priests called out to John, "Are you the Messiah?"

He answered, "I am not he!"

"Are you a prophet?"

"I am not!" John said. "I am the voice in the wilderness!"

"Then why do you baptize? Are you one of those who live in the caves with nothing, crying out that the kingdom of Heaven is at hand?"

"And indeed it is!" John called back. He baptized another and then another as he spoke. "I cleanse with water! He who comes after me will baptize with fire! I will not be fit to work his sandal, and he will baptize with fire!"

The Pharisees asked, "So, he will come to burn us? To kill?"

John said, "Not to burn, but to illuminate! To cast the light of the Holy Spirit on all! And all will be revealed! Some will embrace the light and some will shrink from it! Which of these will you be?"

I turned to Yeshua and said, "I fear your cousin is righteous, but his circumstances have taken his senses from him. Let us not excite him any further, and let us leave before he recognizes you."

Yeshua looked at the Pharisees and then at me. He said, "Let us return tomorrow so that my words with John are for me and John, and not for the priests and the Levites."

With that, the four of us retired to the tents[113] and we ate bread and figs. We drank of the fruit of the vine, with water, for it had become thick.[114] From his bundle, Yeshua pulled his cup. It shone in the light.

"Ah, you still have it," James said.

"I will always have this cup until I pass out of this life. And then, my friends can find me when I return and use it once again in the test," Yeshua said.

"So, you have come to fully accept their ways," James asked.

Magda said, "There is a middle way. You might keep the comfort of knowing that our Heavenly Father knows all and, in his mercy, protects us, while at the same time, we understand that we must end all suffering by learning not to crave, by being kind and gentle to every neighbor, by forgiving every trespass."

---

113 Some sort of temporary shelter, actually.

114 Viscous. Fermentation was used only as a way to preserve, and the porous vessels in which this fermenting juice was stored allowed moisture to escape. "Wine" contained alcohol, but it was often bitter and almost gelatinous at times.

Yeshua said, "But you have, until now, resisted both."

Magda said, "I have not rejected anything, except an absolute choice between the two."

She still amazed me, I wondered at her openly, but I had learned to keep tight my craving. The wound had healed over with tougher flesh, and it was a relief. I found I could once again think in her presence.

The Other whispered, "Denier."

James asked, "So, you believe that we return to live again and again? That this is part of the Lord's design? Should we love everyone? Should we love our enemies? Even the Romans? And should we not crave anything? Not even freedom?"

Yeshua said, "It is only through not craving that one attains freedom."

James asked, "But our Father in Heaven would have us return and live another life as an animal?"

Yeshua said, "The Father would not humiliate us to have us live as something that crawls, but it can take several attempts to live in a righteous way, to reach enlightenment, and we return to help others as well."

James fell silent. He appeared to be considering all this. He turned to me, "You believe this as well?"

"I have accepted more of the path I found in the mountains and in the land of the Sindh, than have I held to the Father. I still believe in the Lord God, but I believe perhaps he watches more from a distance, watches our choices and the outcomes," I said.

James turned back to Yeshua. "Do you, brother, believe you are the Messiah?"

"I am one of many who are anointed. I serve at God's will," Yeshua said.

"But the messiah foretold by Isaiah, do you believe yourself to be he?" James asked.

"We are all sons and daughters of God," Yeshua said.

James turned to me again. "And you believe this as well?"

I said, "I saw the people listen to him. I saw them open their hearts and minds. At last, I felt mine open. Years ago, I came to Jerusalem to escort[115] a student to knowledge; I return with the student become the teacher."

We filled the one cup with wine and water and we shared it. We broke bread and we ate.

*   *   *

The next morning, we set out early to see John once more. We found him alone at the spring. In the distance, a few people slept, scattered about like a small flock.

"I am Yeshua, your cousin."

"I know who you are," John said. He looked at me and said, "And I saw you not long ago."

Yeshua said, "Baptize me, John."

"You come to me? You come to me for baptism? You should be the baptizer! You should baptize me!" John said. His voice grew louder with each word.

"Fulfill the words of the prophets," Yeshua said. "Baptize me now."

"You there! You people! This is the Lamb of God who will take away the sins of all! This is for whom I have made a path! This is the one who will cast light into the shadows, so that all may see!" John said.

"All have light within themselves; they must learn to shed

---

115 Literally, "to ride" and not "to escort," but I found it shaded the meaning in a way I felt was off the mark.

this light for themselves," Yeshua said.

John dipped both hands into the water and wet Yeshua's face. John again dipped his hands into the spring and stroked Yeshua's hair. John began to laugh.

Yeshua placed his hand on John's shoulder, calming him. "You are a son of God, be at peace," Yeshua said quietly.

John spoke past Yeshua to the people who, roused, slowly approached. "This is the son of God! He will baptize with holy fire!"

John and Yeshua embraced and kissed. Then Yeshua stepped away and climbed a stone. He asked the crowd, "What are you seeking?"

Voices shouted. "The Messiah!" "Isaiah!" "A way to drive away the Romans!"

"What are you seeking?" Yeshua asked again. John began leaping in place and laughing.

A voice cried out, "Wisdom!"

Yeshua's eyes fell upon the man. "What is your name?"

"I am Andrew," he said.

"Andrew, I am staying in a camp this night and tomorrow I go to Galilee. Come with us," Yeshua said.

"I will. I will fetch my brother. We are from the north shore and will go with you," Andrew asked.

23

That morning we were to set out for the home of James when Andrew returned and pulled a man to Yeshua.

"This is my brother, Simon," Andrew said.

"A Greek name and a Hebrew name in the same house," I said.

Simon was a large man, solid. His hands were enormous, even larger than those of Menelaus. "Our father is called Jonah," he said.

Yeshua asked, "So you would follow me? For your brother?"

Andrew said, "Not for me, I told him that you are the messiah, that you are the Lord's chosen one."

Yeshua said, "And Simon, you believe your brother so completely?"

Simon said, "I want to believe and so I am here. I trust my brother."

"And, Andrew, do you trust your brother?" Yeshua asked.

"I trust him for he is as constant as the stone," Andrew said. "He is steadfast."

"Simon, son of Jonah. I will call you Kepha[116] and you will be constant for us as well. I will assemble a party. I came here with Thomas and Magda. I would assemble a party just as Jina did, of eleven men. I would that you and your brother would be the first to join us," Yeshua said.

I thought of Padavan. His dedication to Jina's teaching. I was not sure if I could become that dedicated to Yeshua. I would follow him, but I knew him when he was young and the craving for Magda that I had buried might foul my devotion.

"I came to see. Still, we have to work on the sea. The catch. My wife and her mother depend upon us for the catch," Simon said.

"Come with me. Help me find the last nine men. Become fishers of men," Yeshua said.

"How will we know which are the right men?" Andrew asked.

"Man is like a skillful fisherman, casting his net into the sea and drawing it out full of small fish. If the wise fisherman finds among them a large fish, he throws the smaller back into the sea, having selected the largest," Yeshua said. "Do you understand? Do you, Kepha?"

Simon Kepha said, "I understand. There is one in Bethsaida I would catch. He is practical and learned. We will fish for men."

"And no women?" Magda asked.

"Perhaps women," Yeshua said.

"She should leave us," Simon Kepha said. "Who is this

---

116 *The document is written in Greek, but they were not speaking Greek. Instead they were speaking Aramaic. While the document indicated that Simon would be called "Petros," it is obvious that "Kepha" is more appropriate since that is the Aramaic word for "stone." It is unlikely that Simon was ever called anything that sounded like "Peter."*

woman who speaks this way? If women are members of a cause, the cause is cast into doubt. Is a woman worthy of the messiah?"

Magda's fists clenched and she approached Simon as if to say something, but it was Yeshua who spoke.

"She follows the path. She is a living spirit. She may return as a man. We do not know what path is chosen for us, in this life or in the next," Yeshua said.

I could see that Simon was unconvinced, but Andrew seemed to have no worries. What I knew to be true was that Magda would be the last person Yeshua would choose to exclude.

We departed for Galilee and made an uneventful journey. The two brothers did not say much, not even to each other, for Simon told his brother to be quiet. We left James at his house and we traveled north, to the home of Simon Kepha. There the brothers left us, with the wife of Simon and her mother. They soon returned with a man. He was Phillip, whose Greek was always the best of all, and he knew their ways.

Andrew said, "This is the man. This is Yeshua, who is the messiah and who will lead us. We will go with him, and we will gather unto him another eight men, and we will tell of him to all who will listen."

Philip said, "But I have a home with a wife and three daughters."

Yeshua stepped forward. He placed his hands on Philips shoulders and said, "Follow me."

"Tell me where you are from. Tell me who you are," Philip said. "Are you the messiah, as Andrew claims?"

"I have a mother in Nazareth, where her honorable husband Joseph died, and I grew to a man there, but I am one who is of the whole world. I am one who trusts the prophets and knows our Holy Father, and one who seeks to end the suffering in all the world. I am one who knows this and follows the path to enlightenment, and would see the low lifted, for all are equal in the eyes of the Lord. I am one who shall give you what no eye has seen, no ear has heard, no hand touched, no mind has conceived, nor any heart received," Yeshua said.

Magda looked at me and smiled. My heart warmed with the truth of his words and knowing of her smile. I felt lifted. We would live simply, we would remain humble, but we were setting out on a great adventure.[117] The brothers stood by, and while Simon Kepha was stolid, Andrew seemed as if he might scream with his energies.[118]

Philip heard these words and said, "I will follow you."

We stayed there until James, Yeshua's brother, whom we came to call James the Just, sought us out. He said to Yeshua, "There is a wedding. You must come. Your mother and brothers and sisters will all be there. Let them see you now."

"We are a small band now," Yeshua said. We stood together, we six.

James looked at us. "You may all come."

Magda said, "Let me see your mother and your brothers and your sisters."

Yeshua said, "We will go to the wedding. Where will it be?"

James said, "In Cana."

---

117 *This is reasonably close.*
118 *As awkward as this wording seems, you must trust that I have given the reader only a glimpse into how challenging this effort has been.*

24

When we arrived in Cana, we saw a man studying the laws. He was young, with black hair, and Philip knew him.

"May I ask him to join us? He is wise beyond his years, and he is a happy man," Philip said. Philip walked to the man who left his reading and they returned. As they approached, we could hear them speaking.

"We have found him of whom Moses wrote in the law and about whom the prophets wrote. He is Yeshua, a man from Nazareth," Philip said.

"Can anything good have come from Nazareth?" the black-haired man said.

We laughed, save for Simon Kepha. Even Yeshua laughed at his remark.

"Come see for yourself," Philip said.

Yeshua said, "Now there is a true Israelite who hides nothing."

"How do you know anything about me?" the man asked.

"Before Philip went to get you, I could see you inside, reading the law," Yeshua said. "We all saw."

"Well, then, you must be the messiah," he said. "My name

is Nathanael bar-Talemai."[119]

"Because I saw you reading, you believe?" Yeshua said, and he smiled. "You will see and hear greater things than that if you follow me. You will come to see the heavens opened, you will see the sons and daughters of man lifted."

Nathanael and Philip walked together, as did Simon Kepha and Andrew. Yeshua walked with Magda, and I with James the Just. We came to the wedding and Yeshua sought out his mother. His brothers and sisters were there, as James had promised. Miriam greeted me warmly. She had aged little, it seemed, since last I saw her.

"Mother, this is Magda," Yeshua said. He did not introduce any of the men. His sisters immediately gathered around Andrew as he was pleasing to them. Magda bowed to Miriam. I had never seen her do anything so deferential before. She had nearly challenged Simon Kepha but now she gave [indecipherable] to Miriam.

"Come into the crowd, and eat," Miriam said.

We joined and with time, we separated. When next I saw Yeshua, he was speaking with his mother in hushed tones.

"But they have run out of wine," Miriam said. "This will be shameful to the bridegroom and his family."

"What has that to do with me?" Yeshua asked. "This is not my wedding."

I walked over to six earthen jars that smelled of wine. They appeared as wash water jars, but were not. Looking inside, I could see the thick remains of wine along the bottom.

"Yeshua," I said. He approached. I said, "This is wine here. Perhaps the servants are unaccustomed to wine in such

---

119 So we have here the proof that the apostles referred to as
   Nathaniel and Bartholomew are actually one single man. The
   two names are, in essence, his given name and his surname.

large quantities and do not know."

"Mother, have them put water in these jars," Yeshua said.

Miriam turned to the servants, who stood surprised, and said, "Do whatever he tells you to do."

The jars were filled to the brim. As we watched, the water turned red as the wine became one with the water. The servants gasped. "Is it good enough for a wedding?" they asked.

Yeshua said, "Bring some to the director of this feast. Have him judge it."

We followed and watched the tired man drink of it. He looked past us and called the bridegroom to him and said, "It is usual to serve the good wine first and then the lesser wine, but you have kept the good wine until now."

"Bring some to all who want of it; I have brought six jars, each with two measures[120] of good wine and there is plenty for all," said the bridegroom, and then he walked away.

The servants were amazed and went forth, claiming Yeshua had changed water into wine. We smiled at it. Especially Nathanael, who said, "You have lifted many sons and daughters here."

We smiled, but Yeshua was not sure.

"What have I begun?" he asked me.

I looked to Magda, who was smiling with Andrew and Nathanael, and I said to Yeshua, "Come away with me. Let us go to the wilderness and seek a quiet. You will decide anew what we hope to accomplish and I will give whatever counsel I might."

Yeshua agreed to this and so we left Magda with James the Just and the others and we retreated to the wilderness.

---

120 Perhaps 20 gallons.

25

We went into the wilderness for many days and many nights and ate very little more than figs and honey.

We spoke of many things we had seen together in the land of the Sindh, we spoke of Dawa. We spoke of the Shudras, and of how the downtrodden in the east were more openhearted than the low of our homeland.

"It is perhaps because those oppressed in the east are oppressed by their own, oppressed in spirit, and have come to accept their lot. Here, the poor and the weak see outsiders as the oppressors, and they see inequity, and they reject it. With that rejection comes craving and so they suffer," Yeshua said.

"So we would have them accept the Romans and we would have them not crave to be free of Rome?" I asked.

"Once free of Rome, they will crave something else. They will turn on each other. See how they do not divide what they have to help a neighbor as the Shudras did. Free of Rome, they will also be free of what joins them, and they will split," Yeshua said. "There is no peace. They will have strife for an age," Yeshua said.

I thought about this. I said to Yeshua, "Do you not crave anything?"

He looked into my eyes. "I have her already."

That craving which I had hidden from myself came rushing to my mind and heart and spirit. The Other rushed into my front.[121] Never before had he taken voice, until now.

"We are hungry. If you really are a son of God, if you truly are an anointed one of God, command this stone to change into bread," the Other said. I had never heard his voice in this way before. It was frightening—part growl, part song.

Yeshua replied, "Bread is not the most important when it comes to survival."

The Other said, "You could be king of all the lands. The people will rise up wherever you go if only you would command them. You need not suffer fools any longer. All you need do is to relent, and accept your cravings, let them guide you."

"Get this behind me. I will be guided only by the Lord our God, my holy Father, through whom all peace comes," Yeshua said.

The Other raged. "I would throw you from that peak! And if you are a son of God, you would be without injury for it is written that the messengers of the Lord will bear you up and you will not so much as dash your foot upon a stone!"

Yeshua said, "It is also written that one must not test the Lord. Throw me if you must, and what will be, will be. I expect nothing. Be gone from Thomas, whom we love dearly. Be gone and give us peace."

The Other left me, but he did not go far.

Yeshua said, "Let us return to Galilee and continue our teaching."

---

121 *To the forefront of his "self," we might suppose.*

26

We soon rejoined James, Simon Kepha, Andrew, Nathanael, Philip, and Magda. We went to Capernaum and he taught on the Sabbath and they were amazed at him. He brought them a message that empowered them.

"We are all sons and daughters of God. We all have a light within us. We must shower all of our neighbors with love. You must share all that you have and covet nothing. Teach yourselves that that which you do not have, you do not want, and you do not need. Give without expectations. Then all of you can be free from suffering," he said to them.

I saw a man, he was seated, watching Yeshua teach, and talking madly to himself. I saw him and felt kinship and pity. The voice can be so loud as to drive all thoughts away. Yeshua approached him and the man cried out in a loud voice, "Do not come to me! Away! What I do means nothing to you, Nazarene! Have you come to destroy us? I know you! You are the anointed one of God!"

"Be silent and come out of him! Leave him as one!" Yeshua said. The man leapt into the dust, with many astonished around him. He was not hurt and when he spoke, it was with an entirely different voice.

The people questioned, "How was this accomplished? Does he invoke the power of God that he might command unclean spirits?" From there, his fame spread.

*   *   *

We returned to Nazareth.

It was the next Sabbath and we went to the synagogue and he read the words of Isaiah from the roll. "With the Spirit of the Lord upon me, because He did anoint me to proclaim good news to the poor and sent me to heal the broken of heart, to proclaim to captives deliverance, and to the blind deliver sight, to send away the bruised with deliverance, to proclaim the acceptable year of the Lord."

Yeshua folded the roll and gave it to the steward[122] and then he sat down, with everyone looking at him, and he began to say, "Today, the words you have just heard, the prophecy is fulfilled."

I listened as they spoke well of him. They marveled and said, "Is this not Joseph's son?" They admired. "How can this be?" They wondered.

Yeshua then said, "No doubt you want me to do here as I did in Capernaum. That I, the physician, should heal myself and my own. But honestly, no prophet is accepted in his home country and it would be the same here. No physician heals those who know him well. For proof, in the days of Elijah, the sky was blackened with smoke and dust and ash for three and a half years and there was a great famine and a great number of widows and Elijah went only to one, Sarepta of Sidon. Elijah cleansed only one leper, Naaman

---

122 Or the official?

the Syrian, though lepers abounded."

At this, the people became angry. I, too, was surprised that he would not help his own village. There were so few there to help. His mother and sisters would remain here, bathed in the anger of the people. Why would he do something like this? They dragged him from the synagogue and we followed. We tried to free him, but could not at first. Yeshua did not resist but walked quickly with the people, toward the cliff. He went so quickly forward, so calmly, that they released his garments and hair. He moved to one side and then slowed within the crowd, which lost him within itself. Truly, I was not sure where he was either. Upon reaching the cliff, they saw they no longer had him, and soon dispersed.

James and Yeshua's mother and brothers and sisters all remained in Nazareth, but Yeshua could not. It was decided to go north to Capernaum and Bethsaida, to the home of Simon Kepha.

Miriam was sad at this. She said, "Magda, I would have you mother him."

Magda said, "I would mother for him."

Nathanael laughed at this. The Other screamed from the recesses of my mind but stayed hidden. Miriam's face was as stone.

Simon Kepha said, "You are all welcome in my house. Come if there is the slightest reason."

James and Simon kissed. In the years to come, they would come to trust each other to the exclusion of others. Especially when the lunatic Saul, remembered to be one of the Pharisees, began his journeys among the Gentiles, calling himself Paul and claiming to speak for Yeshua.

We left in the morning. We made our way through Capernaum and into Bethsaida. When we arrived at Simon

Kepha's home, his wife ran out to meet us.

"My mother is deathly ill with fever," she said.

We entered the home. The first to reach her was Magda. Then all were gathered around the poor woman.

"Out, everyone leave us," Magda said.

Everyone left but Yeshua, me, and Magda, and as Simon Kepha left he asked, "What do you need?"

"Water," Yeshua said. "And cloth."

Simon brought these and left once more.

"Shall we cool her?" I asked.

Yeshua said, "Shut the screen and remove these bedclothes and her garment."

Magda immediately did as she was told. The old woman was laid bare and shivering.

"Good, she is cold," I said. "Why do they still cover a fever with a blanket here?"

"They do not understand that the road to healing is not always a comfortable one," Yeshua said. He began to pour water onto the cloth and stroke her body with it. She shivered all the more. She cried out.

Yeshua tried to explain to her. In a loud voice he said, "The fever must get out."

I applied water also and Magda began to use a blanket as a fan.[123] It was not long before the woman cooled and her eyes opened. She was old and tired, but she spoke and we gave her to drink. This was good. She was kindly and offered Yeshua some of her water. Magda laughed at this, and found a clean, cool garment for the woman and helped her dress.

Simon Kepha's wife came back with Yeshua, and seeing her mother speaking, embraced her and then she went to tell

---

123 Or use cloth to fan, or something along those lines. The passage literally read, "Used the cover to cool."

the people and his fame spread again. Great numbers of the sick were brought to him and he healed a great many and drove out many spirits. This he did throughout the night and when morning came, the number continued to grow.

* * *

Days passed and we traveled and we ate in the home of Martha, Mary, and Eleazar, friends Yeshua had long known, since the days of his childhood. Martha had always been kind to him, he said, and Eleazar had been as a brother. Eleazar, even then, did not appear well.

Mary anointed Yeshua's feet with oil and Magda was displeased.

"We might have sold that oil and fed the poor," Magda said. I knew that she was not displeased because of the poor.

Judas said, "This perfumed oil was worth twice what we have in the purse."

Mary said, "This narada[124] comes from the East, high in the mountains, and I thought to remind you of your time there."

I remembered the scent well. I wished to return to Kapilavastu and I wondered if Magda would go, for she was so displeased, she left the house. Mary's brother and sister did not object to the use of the perfume, and Mary upended the alabastron.

Yeshua said, "You will always have the poor among you, but soon you will no longer have me." He had not even noticed

---

124 Spikenard. Even the Gospel of John supports this. Another connection to India here, since Spikenard grows between 8,000 and 15,000 feet elevation in the Himalayas. These three siblings must have been wealthy indeed.

Magda's departure. He kissed Mary on the head and she ran her oily hands into his hair and they stood.

Magda returned and we ate. She was silent. Eleazar choked. He took a tonic.[125] He did not drink it, but merely rubbed it on his lips.

"Soma?" I asked.

Martha said, "It is. It silences his cough and helps him sleep."

"Use caution," I said. "I have seen it kill. Eleazar should not use it alone to aid in sleep, lest he never wake. Be with him."

There came knocking at the door, and when it was opened, we saw the crowds forming for they knew Yeshua was there and they had brought their sick.

"We must move on again," he said.

"But we've not been here two days yet," I said.

"I was sent to teach, not to be a physician," he said.

Andrew, Philip, Nathanael, and Simon Kepha immediately agreed. There was no need to wonder about Magda, she would follow. That left only me. We would move about in Judea. We knew no one in those places.

"Thomas, I need you to come with me. You have been to the east and you understand," Yeshua said.

"She understands," I said, nodding to Magda.

Yeshua agreed and said, "She does, but none but other women will listen to her. I need you to come with us."

---

125 A best approximation.

27

It was in Judea that we met Judas, son of Simon of Kerioth, and thus known as the Iscariot.[126] He was bright and I found him to be more interesting and of more promise than the fishermen Andrew and Simon, of more joy than Philip, but less foolhardy than Nathanael. As skilled as Philip was with the law, so was Judas Iscariot with the purse of our group. It was Judas who could judge without assistance whether or not a bargain was worthwhile or if it was to be avoided.

A small number of people listened as Yeshua stood atop a small stone wall in the marketplace. Truly, there were a number of others preaching to the crowd with competing versions of the truth. Each stood on his own part of the stone wall and each claimed to be the messiah, save one. Yeshua did not assert that he was the messiah, instead he shared the same message he always had. Most walked past, but a small number stopped to listen, and Judas was among these.

---

126 *Thus definitively ends the myth that Judas was a member of the cadre of Jewish assassins known as the sicarii, which was always implausible in any event since the sicarii only arose circa C.E. 50.*

When Yeshua paused, Judas asked questions. He questioned in a way that made Simon Kepha uneasy, but that engaged Yeshua.

"But teacher, how is it that we can liberate ourselves if our bodies are trapped? Is not the self identical with the body?" Judas asked.

"The body is merely a vessel, the spirit is everything," Yeshua said.

"Then should we all free ourselves immediately by shedding these vessels?" Judas asked.

"A spirit set loose is different from a spirit set free. No act of destruction is liberating. Freedom comes from peace," Yeshua said.

Judas joined us that fateful day. I admit, he was my friend.

We went about and, as John had done, we baptized the people who came to listen. Yeshua did not baptize; he taught. However, we baptized, even Judas did. I wonder now at those baptized by Judas Iscariot and what it meant in the world.[127]

It was not long after that word reached us of the arrest of John, Yeshua's cousin. A man came to us, and he said that John had heard of our baptizing the people and was unconcerned. He told us that John had said that we have what God gives us, and that John had witnessed that Yeshua was the messiah.

"Where have they taken him?" Yeshua asked.

"Herod Antipas has bound him in a prison. John angered Herodias, Herod's niece and concubine, by denouncing their union," the man said.

"More likely, it is because John has the ear of the people," I said.

---

127 At the very least, if he did not, I wonder at the idea. Is a baptism by Judas Iscariot regarded as a curse? No matter Judas's actual guilt, history has portrayed him as a monster.

"But it is nearly Passover," said Philip, although John had not seemed interested in the holy days.

"How might I see John? Or petition for his release?"[128] Yeshua asked.

"It is impossible," the man said. "I have told you all I know now." The man left.

"It is terrible," Andrew said. "Surely the Lord God will free him."

Yeshua stared at the ground. How I wish I could have known his thoughts in that moment, the thoughts beyond his words, when he said, "Each of us has a cup from which we must drink."

We set out for Jerusalem, although we knew already there was likely nothing we could do. When we reached the Nicanor Gate, I showed the stones I had laid with my own hands. I looked in all directions as if I might see someone I knew. Judas and Nathanael admired my work, but Philip scarcely looked. Judas went to his knees to examine more closely stones I had shaped. It was on those steps that we learned the horror.

Yeshua had asked only three people before finding one that had news of John. A woman, small of body and face. "John, the baptizer, is dead."

"Herod had him murdered?" Nathanael asked.

"Herodias had her daughter, the spawn of the marriage to her uncle Philip, dance for Herod and he lusted for her and Herodias promised her daughter to him in exchange for the head of the baptizer," she said.

Andrew became ill, so gentle was he. Yeshua held my shoulder. They were not close, cousins but not close, but I

---

128 *This is the spirit of what the text said.*

know now he likely saw possibilities, any of which might be his own fate. The woman departed and his grip on me tightened until I cried out. His face was as a storm. Never before nor since did I see him so angered, not even when in personal anguish.

On the steps of the temple, he fashioned a whip of cords, and then began to drive the sheep and oxen and any man that resisted. He loosed the doves. The animals upset many tables of coins. Any man who stopped to pick a coin or herd an animal was struck. Yeshua was wild and shouting, "The house of God is to be a house of prayer and you have turned it into a den of thieves!"

The chief priests demanded answers, and shouted at him. "By what right do you do these things?"

"If you answer my question then I will answer yours!" Yeshua replied. "The baptism of John, was the source from Heaven or from men?"

I could hear the priests confer in whispers with one another as many looked on.

"If we say from Heaven, he will ask us why we did not believe," said one.

"If we say from man, the anger of the people will be roused, for they thought him a prophet," said another.

The priests turned to Yeshua and said, "We do not know!"

"And I will not tell you by what authority I do these things!" Yeshua said. "But I will tell you this. A man had two sons and told one to work in the vineyard, and this first son refused at first, but then repented and went to work. The man told the second son to work in the vineyard, and the second son immediately agreed to work, but then did not go to the vineyard. Now, which of the two did the will of his father?"

The priests answered as one, "The first!"

"Truly I say to you that the tax collectors and the harlots will see the light of God within themselves before you do, for John came to you in the way of righteousness and you did not believe him, but the tax collectors and the harlots did. And seeing this, you had no remorse!" Yeshua said.

The priests became excited. I thought we should depart. Simon Kepha pulled at Yeshua's garment. The crowd grew into a multitude.

"The kingdom of God will be taken from you and given to the people who produce the fruit of it," Yeshua said.

It was that day, I believe, that the priests and the Pharisees began to find a way to seize Yeshua, although they feared the people, who from that day were sure he was a prophet. The priests whispered among themselves, but this time I could not hear the words.

Yeshua must have sensed their conspiracy too for, striking his own chest, he said, "Destroy this temple and within days I will raise it up again!"

One of the priests said, "It took forty-six years to build this temple!"

The priest did not understand that Yeshua was speaking of his own body.

The Other came to me suddenly, and in a calm voice said, "It begins."

*   *   *

The next day, Yeshua was teaching a large crowd, perhaps as many as one hundred men and women, when Sadducees and disciples of the Pharisees came near. They had come to trap him with his own words, so that he might be arrested as John was.

Yeshua said to me, "See how like the Brahmana and the Kshatriyas they are? They peer like birds upon these bones."

I said, "It is much the same. You teach the low, and the high come in fear. There is cause for caution, Yeshua."

"But this is why I came. This is why my Father sent me here," he said.

One of the men of the Pharisees called to Yeshua. "Teacher, we know that you are honest, and that you are not in the service of any man."

"Untrue!" Yeshua said. "I am in the service of all men and all women!"

"Teach us, then," the man continued, "if it is lawful to pay tribute to Caesar?"

Philip stepped forward and said quietly. "They mean to have you fall foul of the Romans and have you for a criminal."

"I know," Yeshua said, and then to the disciple of the Pharisees he said, "Show me a coin of tribute."

They brought Yeshua a denari coin. Yeshua asked, "Whose image is this and whose inscription is this upon this coin?"

"Caesar's," the man answered.

"Render the things of Caesar to Caesar, and the things of God to God," Yeshua said.

The people spoke at this, as a low wind.[129]

One of the Sadducees then spoke, "Teacher, Moses said that if a man dies and leaves his widow without children, that his brother should marry the wife. If there were seven brothers, and each died, leaving no children and each in turn marrying the woman and dying, until even she died, to whom would she be married in the rising again?"

"Where you make your error is in not understanding the

---

129 *A rumbling in the crowd? It is not clear how loud this would be.*

writings nor the power of God. In the great rising again, there will not be the wedded nor marrying of any kind. They will all be messengers of God. And read God's own words that say, 'I am the God of Abraham and Isaac and Jacob!' He is not a God of dead men, but of the living people," Yeshua said.

A man of the law, one of the disciples of the Pharisees then tried to catch Yeshua in another question. "Which of the commandments is the greatest among them?" This was expressly against the law, for it is written that all of the commandments are of equal importance. It is no worse a crime to kill a man than it is to commit adultery or to not honor one's mother. All are the same evil in the eyes of the Lord.

"None are greater than the other, as it is written," Yeshua said. "I give you two new commands. First, love the Lord with all your heart, soul, and wit. Second, love your neighbor as you do yourself."

"Surely there is more," said a Sadducee.

Yeshua turned to the people and said, "Share all that you have, do not take what is not given you, do not crave, and suffering shall pass you by. Love everyone, even your enemies. Blessed is the man or woman who has understood suffering, for he has truly discovered life. Forgive everything, suffer everything, and do not crave anything."

A disciple of the Pharisees shouted, "But teacher!"

Yeshua waved him away and said to the people, but in a voice heard by all, "The Pharisees received the keys to understanding, and hid them. They do not unlock the door to understanding, nor enter, nor allow anyone else to enter. They stand outside that door of knowledge and enlightenment; they stand there in fear. Be wise as serpents and as innocent as doves. The Pharisees have seated themselves in the seat of

Moses and repeat the just laws, and so you must follow what they say, but do not do as they do. They say the laws but do not follow. They place heavy burdens upon you, while they adorn their clothing, choose the prime seats at the banquet and in the synagogue, and are called 'Rabbi' by the people in the market."

The Sadducees and the disciples of the Pharisees became enraged and shouted at Yeshua. I thought they might kill him there.

Judas said, "We must away with him."

Yeshua shouted, "Woe to you, Sadducees and Pharisees, who are like a painted tomb! Clean and beautiful on the outside, but inside all unclean, filled with the stuff of dead men! Outwardly you appear righteous, but inside corrupt and full of hypocrisy! Hypocrites who say you would not have spilled the blood of the prophets as your fathers did, but you will torment and crucify prophets and wise men. How will you escape the judgment of the gehenna?"[130]

At this, all were excited and it was no longer wise to stay. We departed and went to the edge of the city where we dined at the house of a widow. She had been the wife of a friend of Philip. She had a young son, who was very curious. He and Yeshua spent long hours talking after everyone went to sleep. Upon waking, with the sun nearly risen, I found them still speaking, much of it about the Buddha, enlightenment, and the path. The boy's name was Mark, or John Mark as his mother called him. He would later attempt an account of

---

130 The place, a valley south of Jerusalem, where human sacrifices had once been conducted. Yeshua here is applying the guilt of past priests to the ones of his time; obviously, he does not mean this literally, but instead just making the association for the benefit of the crowd.

that night, and the stories he was told, but I never saw the boy or his mother again.

It was Nathanael who suggested we return to Galilee. I was not certain that Judas would come with us, since he was from Judea, but he did. Before we left, however, he knew a man who might join us. We went to him, and Simon Kepha was aghast. The man was a tax collector.

"But he is also skilled at calculations and speaks several languages," Judas said.

"Thomas and Yeshua and I speak languages, and will we have so much money that we will need you and him?" Magda said.

"I am not sure that I should follow you either," he said.

"You must come with us. This man is the messiah who will deliver us," Judas said.

"What is your name?" I asked.

"I am Matthew," he said. "How am I to know that this man is the messiah? Why should I have faith?"

Yeshua stepped forward. "That which is easily known, that which is undeniable, requires no faith at all. Does a man have faith that his hands exist? No, because that requires no faith. Without risk, there is no need for faith. We are children of God. What more do you need to know and what is the risk? Follow me."

Matthew listened. "I will go with you."

Judas was happy, but Magda felt we had the wrong sort in our company now.

28

As we sat in a home[131] in Capernaum, the people were a flock against all entry, and Yeshua spoke to them.

"You need not fill the temples with offerings, derived from the sweat of your brow. You fill the temples with hope and patience and love. For the true temples of God are your own hearts. Fill them with love and kindness and hope. And your true offerings are your deeds; for anything that you do to your neighbor, you do to God. And before you look to the temple, be reconciled with your brothers and sisters and all of your neighbors, for this is the way to open your heart," Yeshua said.

The people stared and listened.

Yeshua said, "Respect your women most of all. They are the mothers of the universe and all divine truth resides within them. They are the basis of all that is good and beautiful and just. Upon women depends the existence of all men, for they are the natural and moral support of all. Be submissive toward your wives, for they ennoble you, and by softening your hearts, they separate you from the beasts. Women possess the divine talent to separate good intentions from the evil thoughts in

---

131 Either "a home" or simply "home"

men. Never expose women to humiliation, for you thereby humiliate yourself and lose their love, without which nothing exists. I tell you truly now, any man who oppresses a woman is the furthest from the path and enlightenment, and is held in contempt by our Holy Father."

At these words some men went away, and one was pulling his wife with great force, but many stayed and there was much embracing. I looked at Magda and saw that she was already looking at me. She smiled, and what joy I felt. I knew then that had she chosen me, I would have wrapped her in love and submitted to her and I knew that my heart was a temple to her. And then that joy became pain and I saw that she perceived it and I looked down at the earth.

There was suddenly a clamor and I looked up to see a man being lowered through the roof to Yeshua. The ropes were tied to his mat[132] and slowly he descended until he lay beside Yeshua.

Yeshua placed his hand on the paralytic's leg and then the other. He bent the leg and straightened it. Yeshua pinched the man by the heel and the man cried out.

"Why can you not walk?" Yeshua asked.

"I am too heavily weighed down with sin," the paralytic answered.

"Child of God, your sins are forgiven," Yeshua said.

Two learned men sat nearby and one asked, "Why is he saying such evil words? Only God can forgive sins."

"What is easier to believe? That I would tell this man his sins are forgiven, or that he should rise and walk?" Yeshua asked. "All men and women have the power to forgive sins."

There was a murmuring throughout the crowd.

---

132 *The word in the text is more akin to "couch," but this gives an odd image to modern readers and so I go with mat.*

Yeshua said to the man, "I say you must rise, take your mat, and go to your house. At once! For your sins are forgiven."

The man cried out, with arms outstretched, and rose and walked unsteadily away, and the people were amazed. A soldier of Rome stepped forward through the crowd to Yeshua. He was not of the garrison east of Capernaum, but was a centurion.

"I have come to find you, teacher. I am Lucius Longinus Vitalis. I have a servant, very dear to me, who loves you, and now that I saw you make a man walk, I love you also. I know that you can heal him, for I too am a man with authority. When I tell one to go, he goes. When I tell another to come, he comes. What I tell my servant to do, he does. So, I know if you would just say the word, he would be healed," he said.

One of the learned scribes said, "This centurion is worthy, teacher. His post is in Jerusalem. He has traveled. He helps build the synagogues, and he sees to it that his men are good to our country."

Yeshua said to the centurion, "Truly, I have rarely seen such faith. Go. See to your man, for he is healed." The centurion left at once, praising God.

More people came. In those days, they came from Galilee and Judea and the far side of the Jordan. The crowd swelled, and we went to the sea.

Yeshua turned to Andrew and said, "Find me a boat that I might have some space from the multitude." There were two brothers, friends of Andrew and Simon Kepha. They had all fished together. The brothers were James and John, sons of Zebedee. Andrew and I went and asked them for a boat.

"Just a small boat, which a single man might sit in. It is for our teacher. He would speak to the crowds," I said.

"Andrew, is this teacher the man called Yeshua the

Nazarene, of whom you have spoken and we have heard?" James asked.

"The same," Andrew said. "Come and listen."

James and John looked to their father, who nodded his assent. They left their father there with his hired men. They never again returned to their nets. John went for a small boat, but it was not of Zebedee, but instead one Simon had abandoned some time before.

Yeshua stepped into the boat and Andrew and James pushed it out onto the water. Yeshua sat in the boat and the people sat on the shore and a hush fell over them.

Yeshua said, "Know what is before you. That which is hidden will be revealed."

A man shouted across the water to Yeshua. "Teacher! Should we fast? Should we distribute alms? Should we pray? What rules should be observed when we eat?"

Yeshua said to all, "Do not lie. Do not do what you believe to be wrong. Do not be concerned with observing rules when you eat. A person cannot be defiled by what goes into a body, but I tell you now that people can defile themselves by what comes out of their mouths and hearts."

There were Pharisees in the crowd and one shouted, "We saw your disciples pick grain as they walked through a field, they picked it and rubbed it between their hands, and ate and this was on the Sabbath!"

The Other came and said only to me, "That was you and Judas Iscariot eating the grain. Did you know it was the Sabbath?" I ignored him and looked to Yeshua for his answer.

"Have you not read what David did, when he and those with him were hungry? They entered the house of God and ate the loaves there as an offering. Those loves were meant for the priests alone, but David ate them. I tell you, there is something here more important than the temple. If you had understood the Holy Scripture, you would have understood that the Lord prefers kindness and mercy to sacrifice," Yeshua said.

Magda moved close to me. Arm against arm.

Yeshua continued. "The planter went out to sow seeds. Some fell by the road and birds ate them. Some fell in the rocks, in shallow soil, and did not have much root, so the sun soon scorched them and they withered. Others fell among the thorns and were strangled. Some fell upon good soil and gave a good crop, some indeed a hundredfold, and some sixty, and some thirty."

There was the low sound of voices again and then a man shouted, "Yeshua, explain your stories. Explain the lesson to us!"

Yeshua held out his arms and quieted the crowd. He looked across them all and said simply, "I will not." He lowered his arms and left them to contemplate for themselves. I saw the truth of it. He would let them find the answers rather than give them the answers, since the lesson would more firmly take root in this way. Truly, Yeshua was a gifted teacher. Still, the crowd became so loud that we knew they would hear nothing else then.

As Yeshua came ashore, we tried to decide how to leave. We could not. The people kept us there and we separated in the throng. Guided by the fishermen among us, as the sun set, we made our way into many boats and pushed away. We did not know how many were in the boats and who was left in the madding crowd.

I called out. "Yeshua!"

Simon Kepha called back, "We do not have him!"

The crowd, becoming more distant, began searching for

Yeshua amongst their own. We could hear them. "Where is the teacher? They have left him! He is not in the boats!"

When we landed on a far shore, we could see the people but we could not distinguish one from another. It was then we discovered Yeshua in one of the boats, and we were quieted. Soon we saw the people setting out with torches, walking around that water across which we had sailed.

I embraced Yeshua, after Magda did, and I said, "Remember the story of Sariputta? Buddha's faithful who crossed the river? These people will believe that you walked across the water to get here ahead of them."

Yeshua smiled. "Perhaps I did."

29

The people arrived and they were much surprised to find Yeshua among us. It was dark as they lay all about. Yeshua and I walked among them while the others stayed at the shore. We climbed the grasses, with night light.[133] In the shadows of garments, and from bundles, we glimpsed all manner of food. Many were well-provisioned. Still others had nothing, but those who had some were hiding their [indecipherable].

In the morning, when all were awake, Philip came to me with Yeshua close by.

"There are many hungry among them," Philip said.

Before I could tell what we had seen, Yeshua stepped forward, "Where could we buy bread for so many?"

"We have only 200 denari," Judas Iscariot said from the ground where he lay. His accent caused nearby people of Galilee to look.[134]

---

133 The moon, perhaps?

134 "Accent" is a close approximation. There is no other mention of accents. Presumably, Matthew would have one too? Maybe this was something more like a speech impediment, but I think not. I believe the mention of "people of Galilee" point to his being a regional accent. Perhaps this lent to a view of Judas as an outsider.

"This is a good sum and more than half a year's wages for a man, but that sum will not be enough," Philip said.

A boy close by heard us and stepped forward. "I have some loaves and some fish."

We looked into his basket. From behind, his father hissed at him. Perhaps six loaves and only three small fish.

Yeshua placed his hand on the boy's head and smiled. He took a loaf and a fish and gave it at once to the boy. He took that which was left and moved to a place to be seen by all. "All those who have ears, listen!" Yeshua called.

The people quieted at seeing him.

"You must learn to give. Craving is the cause of all suffering in the world. If you share with those who do not have, you cure the suffering in the world. When you give to those who do not have, then you please the Father," Yeshua said.

"If you have money, do not lend it at interest, but give it to those who cannot repay you," Yeshua said.

Many in the crowd were becoming unsettled. The Other said, "Behold those with the most."

One suddenly stood with a loaf in his hand. Yeshua told him to sit. "Take care not to give to the poor in front of many, for then you garner glory for your act, but you will win no favor in the eyes of the Holy Father. Whenever you do some kindness, do not blow a trumpet like the hypocrites do, so that they might have the praise of men."

The man sat and hid the loaf. There was some noise among the people now. Yeshua raised his arms. "Give in secret. Do kindness in the hidden ways. Your Father Spirit can see your act.[135] Your act will be secret, but you will be

---

135 This is the only place in the manuscript that he refers to a "Father Spirit."

rewarded manifestly, and inside and radiantly."[136]

Next, Yeshua again spoke the words of Buddha. Yeshua said, "Thousands of candles can be lit from one candle without the source being diminished. Joy cannot decrease in being shared."

Yeshua turned to me and John. "Come closer," he said. We went to either side of him. He withdrew a loaf from the basket and tore it. He gave one half to me, and the other to John. "In this way, I reduce the suffering of people, and I share joy, and I am lifted up, and my light is released. Do this and receive the favor of the Lord, and the sins of the world will be washed away."

Yeshua said quietly to John and to me, "Share the bread."

I tore my half into two pieces and gave one to Philip, and John shared with his brother, James. And we each broke the remainders again, and again. Yeshua took a second loaf and tore it and gave a half to Magda and a half to Judas, and they shared in turn. And then, as he knew they would, the people before us, numbering at least 500,[137] began to pull the loaves from their bundles and garments and break them and share them with those who had none until all had some to eat.

"This was truly a remarkable feat," Philip said to Yeshua.

"They have opened their hearts," Magda said.

Those unknown to each other began to speak with one another. No longer were they all there for Yeshua, but they became for each other. Children held at arms length at daybreak ran over the feet of men and women unknown to them and there was laughter across the slope.

---

136 *Not quite "radiantly" but instead having to do with light. Perhaps the internal light of which he so often speaks.*

137 *Rest assured, there is no error here. The number cited in the New Testament is 5,000 but in Thomas's firsthand account, the number was one-tenth of that recorded in the gospels written decades later.*

"Joy has spread and they are lifted," Andrew said. He was excitable.

Yeshua stepped forward with the last of the loaves and shared it. When we went out and collected that which was uneaten, we filled baskets with it. We followed him as he climbed to the top of the slope and there sat beneath a tree and looked down across the joyful assembly. We sat all around him. Yeshua said, "The people of God."

Matthew asked Yeshua, "Are we sons of God? Are we not sons of man?"

"I tell you, there is no difference, for we are all children of man and God," Yeshua said.

Judas asked, "But whom among us are most blessed?"

Yeshua did not look at him, but instead said, "Blessed are the people who have suffered, for they have discovered the true nature of life. Blessed are those hungry for enlightenment, for they will be satisfied. Blessed are the spiritually helpless, for theirs is the kingdom. Blessed are those who mourn, for they will be comforted. Blessed are the gentle, for they will inherit the Promised Land. Blessed are those with a clean heart, for they will be with God. Blessed are those who make peace, for they will be known as children of God. Blessed are those persecuted for the sake of righteousness, for they will reign in Heaven. If you follow my words, and live your life according to the path, there are some who will hate you and hurt you. Know that you are in blessed company, and have joy in your hearts, for they treated the prophets the same way. Be the lights that guide the people, for you will be like a city on a hill that cannot be hidden. Your words and deeds will survive you, so be sure of what you say and do, for you will lead many with your light. Love all, and hate none. Love even your enemy."

James asked, "But what if we are attacked? Can we not resist?"

Yeshua said, "Resist with peace. Defend with love. If you must die, die in a state of bliss. Do not spit on your murderer, but kiss him instead. If you are struck in the side of your face, offer the other side. Do not commit violence on anyone."

I saw Simon Kepha place his hand on his knife. I imagined he felt its weight then.

Andrew said, "I may be too weak for what you ask, teacher."

"Andrew, no one can be perfect, as God is, but you must try. If you love only those who love you, and are only good to your friends, you are no different from anyone. Even tax collectors love their children, eh, Matthew?" Yeshua said.

We laughed, even Matthew.

Simon Kepha, less accustomed to laughing, stepped forward and said, "Teacher, teach us how to pray just as John taught his followers."

Yeshua looked at the earth for a moment. Magda moved closer to him.

Yeshua said, "You may pray in any fashion you feel is true. Prayer must be personal to each, and it is not to be a chorus of voices chanting the same words, for then there might arise a leader of prayer, and that [indecipherable] ill[138] in the eyes of the Father. However, I share my truth in this way. 'Father in heaven, let your name always be holy to me, and may your reign come quickly. May your will be done on earth as it is done in Heaven. Give me bread, day to day, as you did this day. Forgive me as I forgive others. Don't allow me to be tempted from the path.'"

It was a good prayer. It was simple and powerful.

---

138 The word was "ill" and I am unsure how best to substitute, and I believe this word conveys the intent.

"We must make note of this," Philip said.

I could see that Yeshua did not like this, for he had only moments before said that this prayer was his own, but he did not protest.

30

There were eleven of them, for added to our company were cousins of Yeshua's. Two were brothers. The brothers were small men, sons of Mary of Cleopas, the half-sister of Miriam, the mother of Yeshua. The older brother was James, whom we called James the Smaller, for James, fisherman and the son of Zebedee, was a large man. The other was named Judas, whom we called Thaddeus, as I have written. We loved Thaddeus, for he brought laughter to all, and Nathanael loved him most of all. Into the night, we could hear Thaddeus and Nathanael as they whispered and laughed where they lay together. Often, Simon Kepha told them to sleep, as if they were children.

The last of the eleven was Simeon, the staunchest believer of the Laws of Moses, and I was surprised when he joined us, since he was so newly wed. It was at his wedding in Cana that Yeshua had water added to the wine. He was Yeshua's cousin, and should not be taken to have been Yeshua's younger brother Simon, who was still in Nazareth in those days.

Although we were twelve men, when I include myself, we often sat in smaller [indecipherable] together. I often sat with Matthew, Judas Iscariot, Simeon, and Philip. Magda often sat with us as well. We discussed the teachings of Buddha and the path, with complexity and nuance,[139] and although Simeon sometimes became angered, wise as he was, he could entertain ideas with which he disagreed. Simon Kepha, Andrew, James the Greater, and John often sat on the other side of Yeshua. They could carry water and protect Yeshua from the throngs and, in fact, had more than once been required to lift Yeshua out of the arms of the crowd. Then, the remainder that included Nathanael, James the Lesser, and Thaddeus were less students and less laborers but were willing and faithful.

And still with me was The Other. One night, while all slept but for Judas Iscariot and me, he came.

"Repeat what I say," The Other whispered. "Look at Magda."

"You wish me to repeat that?" I said.

"What?" Judas asked.

"Repeat—Look at Magda," The Other said.

"Look at Magda," I said.

Judas looked at her, sleeping beside Yeshua, her head on his arm. "What of her?"

"I have known her as long as he has. I have always been kinder to her than he," The Other said. I repeated it.

Judas looked at me. "You desire her? But she and Yeshua?"

"I have been much more the nurse to her needs," The Other said. I repeated.

"Does she know your heart?" Judas asked.

"She knows. Yeshua knows. And now you know," I said.

---

139 Here it seems Thomas is indicating he was in the more thoughtful group, as opposed to the group that served as what might be seen as a group of laborers and protectors, and a third group that simply believed.

"How can you endure? If you love her, how can you see them together?" Judas asked.

"I love him as well," I said. "All life is suffering because of the craving, and she is one more test for me."

"Weakling," The Other said.

Judas was silent and then said, "It seems wasteful."

"That she is with him?" I asked.

"That he is with her. That he wanders about in villages curing the sick. That he teaches those who cannot possibly understand. He teaches with stories they take literally.[140] He should be in the Temple, in great debates with the Pharisees and learned priests. He could defeat them with his knowledge of the laws, of scripture, with his facility with words, with logos, and with his healing besides. He would be a king," Judas Iscariot said.

I felt a fear creep through me. The Other said softly, "He is ambitious."

I said, "You miss the point of much of his teaching. Remain humble, love your enemies, share everything, and do not crave anything."

Judas said, "I understand perfectly, and only point out that I feel there is much opportunity being left unexplored."

Simon Kepha sat upright. "Be silent. You are no better than Nathanael and Thaddeus. Sleep."

We fell silent and slept.

---

140 *Simplified here for readability.*

31

When we were outside of Judea once more, Yeshua told us that the day would come when he would be taken from us.

Philip asked him, "When you are gone, who among us will lead?"

"None of you," Yeshua said. "Instead, you will go to my brother James the Just."

I heard the breath of Judas Iscariot then. I looked at him and saw his mouth moving even before he said, "But, master, does he know your teaching? Is he more worthy than any of us to lead?"

"Compare me to someone. Tell me whom I resemble," Yeshua said.

Simon Kepha said, "You are like an angel sent from God."

Matthew said, "You are not an angel. You are a man and a wise philosopher."

I did not know what to say, so I said only, "I cannot bring my mouth to utter comparisons. You are a new presence here, something wholly new."

Yeshua said to all of us, "I am no longer your master. I brought a fountain of knowledge and you have drunk what each you can." Then, he took me aside and said three words to me. "Send them away." Yeshua walked to an olive tree and I returned to the group.

Simon Kepha asked me, "What did he say to you?"

"If I told you, you would gather stones and hurl them at me. We will let Yeshua sit apart for a time," I said.

Magda rose to go to Yeshua. I said, "Woman, sit. Leave him to himself."

She stopped and then walked in a different direction.

We all sat and it was then that a boy arrived from Bethany. John asked, "Why do you come?"

The boy said, "Yeshua must come at once, one that he loves is ailing."

I asked, "Who is it?"

"Eleazar," the boy said.

Yeshua approached us. "Death will not be the end of this. Tell his sisters that I have gotten word. Go now."

The boy left. We looked to Yeshua and he said, "We will return to Eleazar and his sisters Martha and Mary."

John and his brother, and Simon Kepha and his brother thought this a poor decision. Simon Kepha said, "But teacher, they want to stone you there. They will kill you, for blasphemy."

Yeshua said, "Because they continue to misunderstand that we are all children of God, and that I am a son of God, and that God is inside us all, and God is inside me and I am one with him. There is a light within each of us and we might light the whole of the world."

James the Greater said, "We cannot go there, for they will kill you."

So two days passed and the boy returned. He spoke only to Yeshua and then departed. Yeshua came to us and said,

"Our friend Eleazar is asleep and I must go and wake him."

Simon Kepha said, "But if he sleeps, he will wake."

I knew what Yeshua knew. It must be soma.

"He is as dead," Yeshua said. "I will go to him." Yeshua began to arrange his bundle.

Magda rose with him. I could not let them go alone. I said, "Let us go with Yeshua, so we might die with him."

At this, Simon Kepha and John leapt to their feet. The last to stand was Judas Iscariot. We walked to Bethany, which took a day. When we found the tomb, we found Martha and Mary and many people there. Martha went to Yeshua and I stopped Mary.

I said to Mary, "Do you, with your nard and your soma, do you have some hing?"[141]

"We do, a small amount, but we do not care for it and it has the most foul odor," she said.

"Run, Mary, as fast as you might and collect it and bring it back here. For your brother's sake," I said.

"But he is dead?"

"Perhaps, but hurry for the hing," I said, and although not a child, she ran.

Many people had come to the tomb from Jerusalem, only perhaps an hour-walk distance, for the women were with means and their brother was thought dead. I went to Yeshua and Martha, where the others stood. Magda held Martha's arm.

"Teacher, had you been here, my brother would not have died. Even now, I know if you ask God for his return, God will grant it," Martha said.

---

141 *Asofoetida, known as hing, is still used today to treat everything from menstrual cramps to diabetes. It also counters the effects of opium, and is thus used as an antidote.*

"Your brother will rise again," Yeshua said.

"I know he will rise in the rising again in the last day," Martha said.

"I am the rising again and I am life. Any who believe me will live again. Any who live and believe me shall never be dead," Yeshua said.

Mary came and fell on Yeshua's feet, the same she had anointed with the perfume before, and said, "If you had been here, he would not have died."

He was moved by the sadness of his friends. Yeshua wept. Mary stood. In her hand, she had a small sack. Yeshua saw it too and looked at me. I said only, "Hing."

Yeshua nodded and turned to Martha. "Have the stone taken away."

Martha said, "But teacher, this is the fourth day. His body will stink."

"You said you believe," Yeshua said.

The stone was moved by three men. There was no odor, save for the hing, and Yeshua said, "Father, I thank you for hearing my prayer." Yeshua then took the hing into the tomb, descending into the dark. I could not see him long, for the steps turned. We waited. Yeshua soon returned.

He stepped out alone, so that I thought truly, Eleazar must be dead, but then he turned and in a loud voice called, "Eleazar, come forth!"

And he they thought dead came out. He was wrapped in grave-clothing and with a burial sack over his head, as was the custom. There were many from Jerusalem who saw this and some fell to the ground in the dust.

Yeshua said, "Unwrap him." Yeshua stepped forward to steady him and the sack was lifted from his head. It was Eleazar. He was unsteady and he seemed quite ill, but he stood. And the people went forth and spread the word, and many came to believe, but it was also then when Caiaphas, high priest that year, heard of this and began to conspire with others against Yeshua.

32

We came again into Jerusalem, with Yeshua on a beast. The people had heard about his healing and teaching and about Eleazar, they thought Yeshua had the power of the prophets, and they cheered for him and lay branches in his path, and their cloaks. Yeshua's sister and mother and her sister were in Jerusalem also and there was joy.

We felt light and love, but there were dangers also, and the priests would try to trap him. The priests and Pharisees brought him a woman, caught in the act of adultery. "Teacher, according to the Laws of Moses, she must be stoned to death," they said.

"Where is the man who sinned with her?" Magda shouted.

"Be silent!" a priest shouted back.

Yeshua bent and scratched in the dirt, and then stood and said, "The sinless among you—let him cast the first stone at her." Yeshua bent and wrote again on the ground.

The priests, looking to both the sinner woman and Yeshua, left one by one. Yeshua asked her, "Where have your accusers gone? Did not even one judge you?"

"Not one," she said, her voice still thick with the tears of fear and shame.

"Neither do I judge you. Go and sin no more," Yeshua said.

Eleazar, who came with us to Jerusalem, was sent back to his sisters for there were whispers of plots to kill him, for he had become a powerful sign. Perhaps the danger to Eleazar made Yeshua mindful of his cousin John, the baptizer, and the manner of his death, and he returned to the Temple and we followed. I was sure in my heart that we would be stoned on the steps, the lot of us. Had he sought my counsel, I would have advised caution. Instead, he stood upon a stone and said, "If only you, O City, had known the opportunity for peace that visits today! But you are blind! The days are coming when your enemies will surround and choke you on every side and tear you down, and your children with you, and leave not one stone upon another, because you did not recognize the light."

The moneychangers and merchants had returned. As before, Yeshua, with far less rage this time, turned over two tables and loosed a number of doves. The people cheered, and they remembered how Yeshua had done this once before. The guards did nothing. Judas Iscariot took false courage from this.

"He is too popular!" Judas said.

"We should use caution," I said.

"Let us go to Bethany and retire," Simon Kepha said.

Yeshua said, "We will dine tonight in the upper room at the home of Joseph of the Gerousia.[142]"

"Teacher, go in and speak with the priests. Come in and

---

142 *The Sanhedrin. A member of the Sanhedrin appears to have been the owner of the house that hosted the Last Supper. Also, his name, unknown before is indicated here as "Joseph" and it is likely that this is the man most often referred to as Joseph of Arimathea.*

speak with Caiaphas, so that he may hear that you are a prophet. So that the high priest might know you," Judas said.

"He does not wish to know Yeshua. He wishes to kill him," John said.

"You were all wrong when you said the people here would stone Yeshua. They have received him with love and adoration. See how the merchant with lost doves raises not even a hand against him," Judas said.

Simon Kepha said, "Enough of this."

Judas said, "Teacher. Let me go find Caiaphas and try to speak with him that I might arrange an appointment with you. I will tell him you are here."

Yeshua stepped to Judas. Their faces were inches apart. Yeshua said, "You do as you must."

I took hold of Judas's garment. "You risk too much. Do not do this."

"He cannot be all that he must if he continues to save one adulteress at a time," Judas said.

"Let him go," The Other said.

"You will not go!" Andrew said. He also took hold of Judas.

"Release him. He does no more or no less than he is meant to do," Yeshua said.

We released Judas Iscariot and, slowly at first but then more quickly, he walked deeper into the Temple. If I had known what would come, I would have struck my friend dead on the steps that I helped shape so long before. Instead, I followed him.

33

As chance would have it, Judas was able to easily find Caiaphas as he was walking with other priests, and when I came to them.

"I would gladly meet with Yeshua to discuss any of this and more," Caiaphas said.

"Do you hear, Thomas?" Judas said to me.

"I think we should have discussed this further before bothering the high priest with it," I said.

"Nonsense. It is no bother. Go back to your master and tell him I would meet with him, here at the Temple, on the second day of next week," Caiaphas said. His manner was pleasant, but I still had great anxiety.[143]

"We will tell him," Judas said.

"I doubt he would be available for a meeting so soon, since it will take us until the appointed day to reach Yeshua," I said.

Caiaphas smiled. "Come now, we know your teacher is here in Jerusalem. Go, and tell him that I would speak with him in four days from now."

The priests left us. Judas was excited, and still not cautious.

---

143 *I have imbued Thomas with insight that perhaps he did not have, but I feel it aids the narrative.*

"Can you not see the dangers that may be present in this?" I asked.

Judas Iscariot said, "Yeshua is the Messiah, Thomas. What harm can come to him? Is it not written that God's messengers will keep him, and bear him up, lest he strike his foot on a stone?"

I remembered how The Other had said these words to Yeshua when we were in the wilderness. The Other and Judas were not so separate. Judas and I parted.

34

Judas Iscariot was not the last to arrive, but he was late to the table. We sat on all sides, Yeshua and the eleven men he selected, Magda, and me. She sat to his right side. On his left was James the Greater, and then I sat next. The last to arrive was John, who was not present but for the very last of the meal. When Yeshua said that one had betrayed him, I confess I believed it might be John, for he was absent. I was wrong.

"One of you has sealed my fate," Yeshua said.

"It was not I, was it?" Simon Kepha asked. The man was sincere, and fearful, since he was often confused and believed he might have done some unintentional thing.

Yeshua said, "It was he who washed his hands in the bowl with me."

Simon Kepha said, "Whoever it was, he will wish he was never born!"

Judas Iscariot, I realized, was the one. I could see on his face that he, too, recognized of whom Yeshua had spoken.

"You do not mean me, teacher?" Judas asked.

"You spoke to them," Yeshua said.

"To arrange an appointment!" Judas said. "Not to betray you, but to enlarge you!"

"Your arrogance has killed me," Yeshua said.

"Thomas was there!" Judas protested.

I said nothing. I realized that Yeshua was correct.

"Caiaphas said he would speak to you in the week," Judas said.

"They make arrangements to come even now. You were followed to this place, Judas, and then our place was betrayed," Yeshua said. "Tell old Joseph below that he, my sister and my mother and her sister, and his family and servants must quit this place."

Judas rose and went to warn Joseph. He left without looking back. I would never see him alive again. John entered then and joined his brother, who quietly told him what was happening.

"Will we wait here?" asked Philip.

"We will eat and then we shall go to the gardens," Yeshua said.

"Surely we have no time to waste," said Nathanael.

Simon Kepha rose and said, "James and John, let us get our master away to safety."

Yeshua said, "Sit, Kepha, sit. We will eat." Simon Kepha sat and watched as Yeshua lifted unleavened bread. No one touched the food before him or her; all watched. Yeshua closed his eyes. "All came together to make this food. Countless beings gave their lives and labor that we may eat. Let us not eat for joy or fattening, but only to dispel hunger and may we be nourished so that we might nourish life."

I recognized the blessing, of course, but none of the others did.

Yeshua broke the bread. "I eat this, so that it will become my body." He then pulled the golden cup from his bundle. He poured wine into it. All the days in one cup! I remembered the first time I saw it and I thought of Dawa and the test, and old Joseph and Miriam. "I drink this, so that it will become my blood." He drank. He shared the bread as he had that day on the shore when teaching the crowd to share what they had, and then passed the cup.

Magda was the first to eat and drink. I came over and sat behind them.

"Should we depart?" I asked.

Magda did not respond to me, and instead asked Yeshua, "What are these men like?" She was worried too.

"They are like children settled in a field that is not theirs. When the owners of the field approach them, and order, 'Give us back our field!' they will be helpless before them and will surrender it," Yeshua said.

The others began to sing a hymn. I did not know it well but some of the words were, "The Lord is God, and he has made his light to shine upon us."

Yeshua interrupted at this and said, "Not upon us, but instead it shines within us!"

The men stopped singing.

Yeshua said, "Listen, all of you. You will scatter[144] tonight, for it is written that if the shepherd is struck down, the flock will scatter abroad. Those who might, we shall meet again in Galilee; look for me there."

Simon Kepha said, "Though the others may scatter, I will stay at your side."

"Kepha, you will deny knowing me thrice before the cock crows," Yeshua said.

"I say I will stay at your side, even if it means I will die," Simon Kepha said.

---

144 *This is the closest word.*

So said we all. We adjourned. It was into my pack that the golden cup of Yeshua went. We went out to the Mount of Olives, to a place known for the oil presses,[145] a garden there.

There a man came, one I knew from the market, and he warned us, "A great crowd comes from the elders, and they have one of your own among them."

"Judas, the traitor," Matthew said. I was surprised at this harshness, for this same Judas had brought Matthew into the circle.

The man said, "They beat him as they go, from his beard and head they rip."

Yeshua told all of us to stay where we were, but then took Simon Kepha and the sons of Zebedee, the largest and strongest of us, into the shadows a short distance away. He spoke to them and I could not hear what he said, but he continued some steps further and then fell upon his face in prayer. Magda and I ran to him. We ran past Simon Kepha and the other two who did nothing to slow us. She placed her hands upon his head.

"I have such sorrow that it alone may kill me," Yeshua said.

"Yeshua, let us leave now. We can return to the east, the three of us. We will leave this very minute and we will not stop until we stand in the rivers of melting mountain ice," I said.

"Leave him and go yourself," The Other said.

Magda said nothing. She only wept at his pain.

"If this cup could pass from me, I would not drink it, but what will be, will be. The will of our Holy Father will decide all. I commend my body into his hands," Yeshua said.

---

145 Gethsemane, from the Aramaic for "oil presses."

"We will stay with you," Magda said.

"I wish to be alone. To pray and to think, to find a peace. Time is short," Yeshua said.

Magda and I left him. As we moved back to the others, we found Simon Kepha, James, and John were sleeping with too much wine from dinner.

"You cannot stay awake and watch over him for an hour?" I said. They woke. Magda and I rejoined Philip, Matthew, and the others.

We heard the crowd approaching not long after, and Yeshua came back to Simon Kepha and the brothers who, it seemed, may have again fallen asleep. We could not tell, but Yeshua seemed to have to rouse them. The people came with clubs and swords and caught among them was poor Judas Iscariot, much abused.

"Whom do you seek?" asked Yeshua. We joined with him as he faced the crowd.

"Yeshua, the Nazarene," said one.

"I am he."

The courage of some of those among them failed and they fell to their knees, but the officers did not and they urged all to stand.

Yeshua walked into their number and went to Judas Iscariot. He said, "I forgive you, Judas." Yeshua then kissed Judas, who wept. At this, the crowd released Judas and seized Yeshua.

"You come for me as you would a robber, with clubs and swords? I sat with you in the Temple and you did not seize me," Yeshua said.

It was then that Simeon[146] drew his sword and struck a man

---

146 n.b. that this is Simeon the Zealot and not the man known as
    Simon Peter

named Malchus above the right ear. How the blood rushed forth! His ear was hidden in it. It was Yeshua who staunched the flow with the hem of a coat. Yeshua said, "No more of this! Put your sword away! Those who live by the sword will die by the sword. If this had been my course, I would have built a different type of host." The bleeding abated.

They bound Yeshua. Then the crowd began to seize us as well. Two men grabbed Magda, and while I fought to free her, a boy rushed in from I do not know where and aided me. So savagely did he fight to free Magda, howling and biting, that they released her and turned on him. In attempting to hold him, they stripped him of the only cloth he wore and he ran off into the grove naked. In this tumult, Magda and I were able to slip away. We could hear Yeshua pleading for the release of all of us.

"If I am whom you seek, release these others," Yeshua shouted.

I could see many of us slipping away. I also saw poor Judas in the grips of the sons of Zebedee. He scarcely resisted, and his head hung.

To Magda I said, "We will find a safe place for you, and then I will go find Yeshua. By the looks of the people, I believe he is being taken before the Sanhedrin."

"I will go with you," Magda said.

She was so strong-willed, I tried my best to dissuade her, but we went together. Truly, I cried more than she as we went, so sure was I that Yeshua was lost. I also burned with guilt for my part. I knew the pride and the naïveté[147] of Judas Iscariot had brought this to them both, but I might have done more, even with the words of The Other in my ears.

---

147 Best word here.

3 5

It was daybreak before the priests had come together. Yeshua was taken first before Annas, the father of the wife of Caiaphas, for Annas was the rightful high priest then. Still, Caiaphas had the title, for Caiaphas had been appointed by the Romans. I went in, while Magda could not, and was with a few who stood by. I could see that Yeshua had been struck several times about the face since I saw him last.

Annas asked him, "What are you about?"

"I have kept nothing secret and spoke in the Temple and the markets and the synagogues. Why ask me? There are those present who have heard me. Ask them," Yeshua said.

I felt sudden fear and felt as thought everyone there knew I was with him.

An officer suddenly struck Yeshua and asked, "Is that how you talk?"

"If I said something untrue, explain it. If what I said was true, why hit me?" Yeshua said.

Annas said, "Do not strike him."

They took Yeshua to Caiaphas then, and Magda and I followed. There we found Simon Kepha. I, again, could enter where Magda could not and I left her with Simon Kepha. When I entered the courtyard, he saw me, and Caiaphas knew me and he nodded[148] to me. How I wanted to kill him for it![149] Was I a man of his? No!

There were many here and they gave false testimony before the elders. So eager were they to please Caiaphas that they gave shameful testimony at odds with each other. This angered Caiaphas and he rose and said, "I put you under oath of the living God! Tell us if you are the Messiah and the Son of God!"

Yeshua straightened. He said, "I am a son of God."

He had scarcely said the words, "I am" when Caiaphas tore his own garment and then said to the members of the Sanhedrin, "What more testimony do you need when from his own mouth you hear his blasphemy?"

I looked at them all. Tired old men. Weary of responsibility, weary of the people's hardship, weary of Caiaphas, weary of faith. They unanimously condemned Yeshua to death. This would have been by stoning, under the Law of Moses, but Caiaphas had not finished.

They took Yeshua to the home of the prefect, Pontius Pilatus. Magda, Simon Kepha, and I followed once more.

As we walked, Magda whispered to me, "Simon denied knowing Yeshua three times, just as he foretold." I looked at Simon Kepha's face, and it was blank, with eyes like dung. He did not speak.

Caiaphas and the other priests would not enter the prefect's house and defile themselves. They waited outside until Pontius Pilatus came.

---

148 *Some sort of physical gesture.*
149 *This I find out of character for Thomas. A good Buddhist here? Is this The Other?*

"What charges do you bring against this man?" Pilatus asked.

"He is subversive," Caiaphas said.

"So, stone him," Pilatus said. "Why bring him to me?"

"He opposes paying taxes to Caesar and claims to be a king," Caiaphas said.

"That is not true," said Magda.

"It will not matter," The Other said.

"It will not matter," I said.

"He even claims to be the son of God," Caiaphas said.

"Are you a king? Are you the king of the Jews?" Pilatus asked.

"Everyone has said this, except for me," Yeshua said.

"What do you say? Are you a king? Are you the son of a god?" Pliatus asked.

"I am a witness. I have come to spread the truth. Those who love the truth hear me and listen," Yeshua said.

Pilatus snorted. "What is truth? Truth is how we each see it."

Yeshua said, "Truth is unchanging, beyond distortion. Truth, alone, wins. Truth liberates."

Pilatus paused before turning to Caiaphas and saying, "I find no guilt in him."

"This is the one they call Son of the Father, the Messiah! He would be king. Caesar would not be pleased at your leniency!" Caiaphas said.

"And my wife has had a dream that I should spare the innocent man. I wonder which I might displease less," Pilatus said. To Yeshua, but loudly, he asked, "Are you Yeshua, the Nazarene teacher of the sick and lame? Or are you this one who would raise a tumult, this one who would be a god and a king, the one called bar-Abbas?"[150]

The crowd heard this and shouted that Yeshua was the one known as bar-Abbas and was worthy of crucifixion. I looked around us. Simon Kepha said nothing. There were so few people about who had heard Yeshua. Save Caiaphas and his wicked priests, none had been seen in the Temple or synagogues, nor were they followers of the Laws. Most were just bloodthirsty and faithless people who wanted to cheer a man to death for the game of it.

"Bar-Abbas! Bar-Abbas!" they shouted. "Crucify him!"

"He is Yeshua!" Magda suddenly shouted.

I grabbed her to move her away, but too late. A man struck her in the face. Simon Kepha then came to life. Such a rage came from the fisherman that I saw him club down two men, each with one blow. His hand fell again and again and truly I thought each blow had killed yet another man. Sadly, this riot only sealed Yeshua's fate, for Pilatus faulted Yeshua for the disturbance. He ordered his soldiers to bring Yeshua inside where we could not see. He called nearly his entire contingent together, and they were among us, for Pilatus had nearly three thousand soldiers then, and only a fraction was needed to quiet the crowd.

We waited. Caiaphas paced, and the crowd waited and there was some talk. Magda cried for Yeshua, and Simon Kepha had escaped.

Pilatus reappeared and said to the crowd, "Although I found no fault in him, and I know him to be a righteous man,

---

150 *This makes clear that there was no choice between two separate men. Jesus of Nazareth was also known as bar-Abbas, which means Son of the Father. Here, Pilate is asking Jesus which version of him is the true one. Is it the peaceful teacher, or the rabble-rouser who upends the moneychangers' tables?*

I have punished him and will release him. Behold the man!"

Yeshua appeared in a long purple robe, beaten and slow. His face was bloody and on his head they had fashioned a crown for him of jujube branches with the thorns in his skin.

My own heart was broken.[151] The crowd became incensed once more, for they had no pity. "Crucify him! Crucify him!" If only more Jews had been there, and not just their high priest, we might have saved him. I could see Pilatus speaking to Yeshua, but could not hear the words, and Yeshua said nothing in return.

Pilatus stepped to the basin and washed his hands, then held them high, water fell from them. "I wash my hands of the blood of this innocent man. His blood is on you."

The crowd cheered. I felt Magda fall against me. Pilatus waved his hand and Yeshua was taken away to be crucified. I pushed Magda to her feet.

"Listen to me, we must go to Joseph," I said.

"To warn Yeshua's mother that her son will be crucified," Magda said. Her voice failed her at this.

"He is rich, and we need help," I said. "Go directly. I will see if any of the others might be found."

Magda left, and I went to see if I might find at least one of the fisherman, so that my resolve might be buttressed. Instead, I found where the sons of thunder had left Judas Iscariot.

He hung from a tree by his neck. His face was so battered I recognized him from his hair and garments. His innards had been cut out and were hanging from him. Oh, how the sons of Zebedee had misunderstood Yeshua's message. Beneath Judas's feet was the purse of all our money, with perhaps less

---

151 *One must assume.*

than fifty denari left. They had killed him and left the money.

When I got to the home of Nicodemus, I found the women weeping where they had fallen together. Salome, Miriam, her sister Mary, and Magda. Joseph stood near the window.

"Joseph, you and Nicodemus have wealth and wisdom, and I am in need of both," I said. "And there is a man we must find."

36

We waited on the hill shaped like a skull,[152] and we could see the procession coming. No one seemed to question the strange location; it had not been a place for executions in the past. Changing the location of the crucifixion was the first of the requests that Joseph of the Gerousia had made of Pontius Pilatus, with whom he was familiar.

Yeshua carried the cross-member with the help of a man of Libya[153] who was dressed as one who observes our laws. Each man had an end of the wood. There were two others condemned and they followed Yeshua, carrying their own.

Although there was a contingent of Roman soldiers waiting with the crowd on the hill, we could see the lone centurion coming along with Yeshua, as he promised. It was Lucius Longinus Vitalis, the Roman whose servant Yeshua had healed. He was not of the unit on the hill, but was of higher rank than any soldier present.

There was a large crowd following behind the condemned men. Men and women, full of sorrow and wailing. If only

---

152 n.b. not a place littered with skulls
153 My simplification here.

these had been there when the crowd and high priest had called for Yeshua to be crucified.

Yeshua and the two others were placed upon their backs and they were lashed to the timbers. I watched as they drove nails through his wrists.[154]

Yeshua was crying out with each blow. "I forgive them! I forgive them! They do not know!"

Magda and other women lamented. The soldiers began to [indecipherable] the structures then. Three poles lay on the ground for each man, joined by a single metal ring. The soldiers moved Yeshua and lay his cross-member across where the three poles met and attached it to the metal ring also. Then they put a nail through each foot, near his toes, pinning them to the sides of the pole upon which he lay.

Then they raised all three poles at once to a point and Yeshua cried out once more. There was a primary pole and then two other vertical poles behind it.[155] Across the two poles in the back, was a cross-member there only for support. Once erected, Yeshua was nailed to wood that appeared like the letter "tau."[156] My heart was torn. His feet were no higher than my head. His hands were well above his head.[157] Most of his weight was supported by the cords around his arms, but the suffering was real.

The other two men were hung as well. Above each head, a soldier climbed and placed a placard, with a name inscribed. On one was written "Dismas" and on the other "Gestas."

---

154 The word for "wrist" is the same as the word for "hand," and since it is basically "translator's choice," I have chosen based on what makes the most logical sense.

155 A tripod.

156 Greek letter resembling a "T"

157 Some simple deduction here; the cross could not have been much more than twelve English feet high.

When Miriam saw this, her breath was stolen. "The boys from the road to Egypt," she said. "He knew, even then, that he would see them again. He knew this day would come."

They hung a placard for Yeshua, but it did not have his name. It read, "King of the Jews" and it only made the company weep all the more.

The one marked Gestas spoke then. "If you are the Messiah, save yourself and us."

Yeshua said nothing.

The other, Dismas, then said, "Be quiet! For we are thieves and this is an innocent man! Yeshua, remember me when you reign!"

Yeshua said to Dismas, "Truly I say to you, today you will be with me in the paradise."

Then, Miriam touched his foot. The soldier nearby stepped to interfere, but the centurion, Longinus, prevented him. Longinus said, "Leave her, she is his mother. May your mother never know this anguish, but touch this woman and your mother will know loss."

Yeshua looked down at us near his feet. I stood there with Salome, Miriam, Mary of Clopas, and Magda. Yeshua said to Miriam, "Mother, this man is now your son." She released his foot and fell into my chest. I held her. This was the second time she touched me, the first being so long before in Bersabe.

To me, Yeshua said, "Man, this is now your mother." I had never known a mother of my own until that moment, but I suddenly felt, in the midst of that horror, all the love that that means.

Yeshua suddenly cried out, "My God, my God, have I forsaken myself?" I looked up at him, and he at me, and he saw what I was doing with the sponge and wine and he said, "I thirst."

I mixed the wine with soma, provided by Joseph of the Gerousia. It was the same tonic Eleazar had taken. I added an ample quantity. I placed the sponge on a branch of hyssop and reached to his mouth, and this he drank readily. The soma took immediate effect and Yeshua said, "It has been finished." He did not know of the plan, so I was unsure; perhaps he thought I had poisoned him.

His eyes closed and he said, "Father, into your hands I commit my spirit." He became limp and those gathered knew him to be dead. I sent a boy to tell Joseph.

The centurion, Longinus, said, "Truly, this man was righteous."

The other two men, Dimas and Gestas, were still speaking. The soldiers sought to speed their deaths and, with rods, broke their legs. Longinus prevented the breaking of the legs of Yeshua. He said, "Guard these, and let none come near." The soldiers moved all of us away. The women went to the ground and wept as one. I waited.

Soon after, one youthful Roman approached and, moving to Longinus, spoke, saying, "The prefect has had a request for the body of Yeshua, the Nazarene, but is unsure and astonished that the man is already dead. How can it be? He will agree to release the body if you can prove and attest to his death."

I knew that Longinus could not simply do this with a word. He demanded the spear of one soldier nearby, and with expert precision,[158] pierced the side of Yeshua. This was the worst for us. Blood and perhaps some other came forward, but Yeshua did not move nor cry out. Longinus threw the spear to the ground and turned to the young messenger. "Tell

---

158 Obviously.

the prefect that the man is dead, and tell what you saw. The body might be released, at his command."

The command soon came from Pontius Pilatus. Joseph of the Gerousia, and Nicodemus, and their servants came and assisted the women and me as the cross was lowered and we unbound Yeshua and freed his hands and feet. The other two, Dismas and Gestas, were left on their crosses for the birds and beasts, as was customary. The Romans left them as a warning, and the holy days did not matter. Taking down a hung person was very unusual.[159]

We carried Yeshua to a tomb newly carved from stone, acquired by Joseph. There we began to wash his body and placed a separate napkin about his head, as was the way. The two soldiers who had accompanied us soon tired of this and left us. Nicodemus sent all the servants away. In the tomb, only Joseph, Nicodemus, the women, and I remained.

There was much weeping. I said, "Mother, place your ear to his heart."

Miriam did this and fell, without a sound, to the floor. Nicodemus and Mary of Clopas tended to her. Magda, stunned, placed her ear on his chest and began to weep and to laugh at once. This revealed the truth to Salome and Mary of Clopas.

Magda, her heart swollen with understanding, asked, "Have you hing?"

"Yes," I said. "But let us wash him and bind his wounds and not hurry to give him the hing, for he will have much suffering. When he starts to wake, I will give him more soma. We will tend to him and wake him perhaps tomorrow or the next."

---

159 The assertion that the victims had to be removed before Passover is proven here to be false.

"But they will not leave us in peace?" Salome asked.

Then more soldiers appeared, and Mary of Clopas was fearful at the sight. Longinus entered the tomb. He said, "These are chosen men who will guard Yeshua and your work. They are secret men and trustworthy. They will claim to any that Pontius Pilatus has posted them here to keep all away from the tomb."

Miriam stood nearby, on the arm of Nicodemus, and said, "May God bless you."

I said to Miriam, Mary, and Magda, "Get the herbs and the aloe. Get fresh linens and clean garments. Bring clean water. If any question you, tell them you minister to the dead."

"The spear wound?" Longinus asked.

"It will heal," I said.

Longinus placed his hand upon Yeshua's head and then left us, but as promised his men stood watch.

We washed and bound Yeshua's wounds and we wrapped him as if dead with a shroud on his body and the napkin on his head lest misfortune reveal to someone unexpected that we were not treating Yeshua as if dead.

On the second night, there were none there but for me and Magda inside, and the Roman soldiers on guard without. I sent his mother and her sister and Salome to journey back to the home of James, and told them to wait there, for the world was still dangerous. They did not want to go, but they did as I instructed.

"You have given my Yeshua back to us, and I will do as you say," Miriam said.

37

We removed the napkin and folded it beneath his head. Magda and I sat quietly by while we listened to the breath of Yeshua. We held each other and watched him sleep. We were full of love and exhausted and had much of the same account and there, in the tomb, beside where Yeshua lay unmoving, we knew each other.[160]

Before the sun rose, I walked to the opening of the tomb. I heard Magda stir behind me.

I said, "We must move Yeshua. We will wake him and we will move him. I will then go to them. They are at the house of Joseph or the house of Nicodemus. You must come soon after and testify that Yeshua is risen. Perhaps Matthew and Philip will not believe, but if Simon Kepha will believe, that will be enough."

"We cannot. We must depart. We will take Yeshua far

---

160 *Although it is tempting to embellish here, I feel that written in this understated way, the effect is enhanced and that any elaboration or strengthening of the narrative as I have done throughout would only detract from the impact of this shocking revelation. The idea that Thomas and Mary Magdalene "knew each other" as the unconscious Yeshua lay nearby is truly important, with implications.*

from here. Perhaps far into the land,"[161] she said.

"We will. First, we will show them that Yeshua lives and this will fix his teachings. We will then leave this land forever," I said.

Magda said, "He has already been crucified. Would you risk that again?"

"I know there is danger, but his teaching can continue without him if we do this. If we do not, he will be one more dead teacher, soon to be forgotten or his memory misused. He was crucified, truly, but would you have it be for nothing?" I asked.

Magda was angry. "We will ask Yeshua."

Soon I gave to him the hing and we watched as he woke. He twisted in pain and we wept with him. In the first, he had no understanding of where he was nor of what had happened. Magda pushed me away and held him and told him in whispers. I could not hear the words, but how he wept as she spoke! I walked to a corner and sat and was tired.

Yeshua was hardly able to stand and he did not see well. We gave him water. Also, he scarcely had a voice, but he said, "Thomas is correct."

"Let us go far from this place," Magda said. I watched her and I had shame in my heart for what we had done, and I felt the loss of her, for she loved him and was never mine.

The Other said, "Just abandon them. There is nothing but pain here and you risk crucifixion yourself in all this. She is for him. You stand to gain nothing. Abandon them."

"We will let them see that I live, so that the word I have spread might live longer," Yeshua said. "Then, I would go to

---

161 *This remains unclear.*

Galilee, for I must see my brothers and sisters and mother. I then will return to the mountains."

"We should not. What if the house of James is watched? We should leave," Magda said and kissed him.

The Other said, "If you killed Yeshua, could they try you? How can one be tried for the death of a dead man? And you could take the woman."

"Enough," I said.

"We will do as I said." Yeshua sat erect.

Magda said nothing. I am sure that she knew how resolute he was. After all, the three of us had been together for many years. And she was his companion.

Yeshua said to me, "Magda and I will go to the house of my cousins[162] for none are there until the season.[163] You go ahead and be among Simon and James and the others. Magda will come to testify. Return with her, ensuring none follow you."

"They murdered Judas Iscariot," I said.

"The crowd?" Yeshua asked. He closed his eyes.

"James and John. They felt he betrayed you," I said.

Yeshua said nothing for some time, but then said, "Let them see me and then we will depart from this land."

---

162 *Familial relatives of some sort.*
163 *As clumsy as this seems in English, I assure you it is far better than the original.*

38

I sat among them and all was mourning, and I ached to tell my comrades that Yeshua lived, though he would not be staying among them. No one spoke of Judas Iscariot, and James and John sat apart. None were as sure as they had been.

As I spoke to Matthew and Philip, Magda arrived. She was breathless, and shouted, "I have seen our lord!" I rose to prepare myself, and the others gasped and gathered round her. She told the story.

Magda said, "I came early to his tomb, before light, and the stone was moved! There, in the tomb, his body was gone! As I came out, I found a man, who said to me that Yeshua is risen from the dead, just as was Eleazar! That I must come and tell all of you, I must tell you Simon Kepha."

Matthew did not believe and said, "His body has been stolen."

Magda said, "I have not finished. Yeshua appeared to me."

All were on their feet. This was the critical moment. Simon Kepha said, "Magda, we know that Yeshua loved you above all others. Tell us what he said, so we might know."

Magda said, "He called me and I knew his face. I ran to him, but he said that I must not touch him, for he has not ascended yet to our Father. Yeshua said he will come to you here, tonight, and then we will all leave Jerusalem in pairs and meet in Galilee."

There were many voices until Simon Kepha quieted them. Magda continued then and said perhaps more than she should have. "Yeshua told me that you do not need priests or any intermediary between you and truth and enlightenment and God. Yeshua told me that you would go out among the peoples of the world and teach what he has shown you. Yeshua told me to tell you that he is nothing more than a man, just as all of you are men, and that all of you can end the suffering of others and do all that he has done. That each of you have it within you to reach a state of awareness that is without structure and is peaceful and without the suffering caused by greed, envy, fear, and delusion."

Simon Kepha became angry. "Why would Yeshua tell all these secrets to a woman, and not to all of us?"

Magda said, "Simon Kepha, would I create this story? Would I tell something untrue about Yeshua?"

I said, "These were not secrets. These same Yeshua told to us all along. Some of us listened more than others." Simon looked at me, as did James and John.

Matthew said, "If the teacher made her worthy, who are you to reject her? He loved her more than he loved us. It stands to reason she would know more than we."

Philip said, "It is true. She was his companion and his partner."

Andrew said, "Let us go to the tomb."

Simon Kepha and I led the way. When we arrived, we found all as it was left. The linens were wrapped together and the napkin that had been around his head lay apart from the rest, folded. They were all amazed. After some time, we all departed. Magda and I went to where Yeshua was staying and we told him all that had transpired.

Magda said, "They did not believe in the first, but they wondered at your empty tomb."

"Thomas, stay with Magda, and I will go to them," Yeshua said.

"Can you go alone?" Magda asked.

"I am safer alone. Moving in a group would draw the eyes of others, but alone, no one will notice me," he said. "Stay with Magda and I will return soon."

I felt guilt at his trusting me with her. I resolved to earn that trust once more.

Late evening, he returned. He charged me. "Thomas, go to them, and see their reaction to my visit and my words."

I went and they would not let me in, for fear in the dark. When finally Matthew opened the door and they saw it was me, Andrew and John spoke first. They said, "We have seen the teacher! He is risen, as Magda said!"

I pretended to not believe. I said, "You must be mistaken. I believe his body taken by the Romans or perhaps the men of Caiaphas."

"We tell you," said Simon Kepha, "it was Yeshua, risen from the dead!"

"Use caution, Thomas, for he was displeased that we did not have faith when Magda came and told us," said James, the son of Zebedee.

I said, "I tell you if I do not see the marks of the nails in his hands, and put fingers to those marks, and put my hand to his side, I will not believe it was him."

"As you wish," Simon Kepha said.

They made ready to depart.

"Do you leave tonight?" I asked.

"In the morning," said Simeon. "We return home."

"For some of you it is home," said Matthew. "We all will go to the home of James the Just, in Galilee."

I spent the night with them and returned to Yeshua in the morning. I found him in the arms of Magda as they slept. I left them as they were, and when he woke, I told him all that had happened. We prepared for the journey to Galilee.

39

We gathered in the home of James the Just. Magda, Miriam, Yeshua's sisters and brothers, the ten of them and a new man, Matthias, and I waited. Simon Kepha locked the door in view of all and I unlocked it, unbeknownst to any. When Yeshua arrived, he quickly entered and closed the door and many were amazed.

"Peace be with you!" he said.

His mother was first to him, and his brothers and sisters. They had not heard his voice until then and at our word that he was coming, they had become anxious. They wept as a family weeps. Magda wept at watching them.

Yeshua had some pain yet, as it had only been eight days since he left the tomb. He turned to me, as arranged, and said, "Bring your fingers, Thomas, and feel the wounds in my hands. Put your hand to my side, and believe."

I did this and said, "My master, it is you! Blessed be God!"

"Having seen me, Thomas, you believe. Happy are those who have not seen, but believe," Yeshua said. I embraced my old friend.

We sat and ate. From my bundle, I removed Yeshua's golden cup, and gave it to him. He did not fill it, but put it among his [indecipherable].

When we had eaten, Yeshua spoke to them. "You must go out, away from me. You must go out and tell all that you have learned. If I can teach ten men, and each teach ten men, who each teach ten men, our number goes to one thousand and grows more beyond."

"But where shall we go?" Simon Kepha asked.

"I, too, would leave this place. I must leave," Miriam said. "While my other sons are staying, I would leave the land that had my first-born nailed to a tree."

"James the Just, my brother, will lead in Jerusalem. Refer all questions to him after I am gone," Yeshua said. "Others will go where according to the lot he draws."

In this way, lots were cast and with his interference, my lot fell to return to the land of the Sindh, but then to the south, far from the mountains where I wanted to live out my days shaping stones.

"You and Magda and Miriam will all to Kapilavastu without me then," I said.

"My mother will go with Philip," he said. I was surprised, as was she. If she was not to go with Yeshua, I thought she would come with me, because he had given her to me as my mother, but these had been the wishes of a dying man. Philip would be traveling north, which was wise since he spoke the language so well.[164]

"We will set out. We will never again be together as we are now. It is too fraught with peril. Know, however, how deep my love is for each one of you. I will go to Jerusalem, go to the market to arrange passage for Magda and me. Go out, spread the truth, and help to end the suffering of

---

164 One assumes the language is Greek.

as many as you can and the Father will smile upon you," Yeshua said.

As he said, we went to Jerusalem. Yeshua and I went to the marketplace. There, as it happened, Yeshua met a merchant named Abbanes, sent as a purchaser and agent by King Hyndopheres. Yeshua sold me as a servant to this agent for a quantity of unstamped silver, which he had no right to do, for I was not a slave. The price paid, Abbanes and Yeshua approached. Magda was in the distance. I remember how she looked at us as they came to me. Abbanes asked me, "Is this man your master?"

"He is," I said.

Abbanes said, "I have bought you. Be here in the morning. We will set out." Abbanes walked away.

Magda approached, but still at a distance.

"How could you do this?" I asked.

Yeshua said, "You laid with Magda while I lay in my tomb. I could not move nor speak, but I could hear you and I forgive, but you must go with this man and leave us. I give you the price of your purchase." He gave to me the silver. "Go shape stones, and shape men and women with the truth. Know that I love you."

I was heartbroken. Magda was with us then.

I said, "He knows."

"I know that he does," Magda said.

"Do you know he has sold me as a slave?" I asked.

Magda was shocked. "Undo this!"

"I cannot," Yeshua said. He reached his hand for Magda, but she withdrew.

"I leave tomorrow as I was purchased and will now go work for some distant strange king," I said.

"Undo this bargain, or you will lose me. I cannot be with

you knowing that my actions led to this man's servitude," Magda said.

Yeshua said softly, "Do what you will."

Magda looked at him and then at me. I could not bear her gaze and looked at my feet. She stepped to me, and kissed me, and then walked away.

"Is this how you would betray me? With a kiss?" Yeshua asked her. She never looked back, but I could see her shudder with tears as she went. I never saw her face again. I doubt Yeshua ever did either. We parted.

The next day, I rose, intending to go immediately to Abbanes. Instead, I sought out Yeshua. He looked as if he had not slept. We found a quiet place and we sat and tried to find harmony together, as we had long before, when we sat with Dawa and we three had known peace and happiness. When we parted, we had peace in our hearts and forgiveness.

"Will you try to find her?" I asked him.

"I will go east and struggle to crave nothing," he said. His smile was pained. We parted, and I joined Abbanes to begin our journey.

IV

No excellent soul is exempt from a mixture of madness.
—Aristotle

Translator's Notes

As unsatisfying as Magda's sudden departure from the narrative may be, I resisted embellishing that scene. It is true to the original document as it is.

It is one of the truly painful elements of doing translation work that the writing, while ancient and worthwhile, sometimes leaves us wanting for additional details, and facets of what we regard as "good writing" today simply were not imperative to storytelling in centuries and millennia gone past.

What follows is the narrative that covers the time post-crucifixion and after Thomas's return to India, including some new historical evidence I am sure will be worth further investigation.

40

We arrived after travel over land and sea, and we found ourselves at the celebration of a wedding, although we were strangers. The king had decreed that any who did not accept his invitation, even strangers, were to be arrested. We went and there was dancing and food and drink, but I had none of it. I sat and watched. There was a woman who played a flute who, like me, had come from Jerusalem. Many people watched me and I said little. They put their perfumes on me and there was laughter. The flute-woman played near me, over my head, and did entreat me.

"Take her, for she offers herself to you and this is a place of merriment. Take her to one of the [indecipherable] around us," The Other said.

"I will not," I said.

But when she finished her song, she laid beside me. I thought of the night with Magda, whose absence I felt, and I knew I always would. And my friend Yeshua. And the shame. And the flute woman plied me with drink and soon we retired to a chamber, and I was upon her, with kisses, when a wine-server came and abused me for lying with her. He struck me, and while I wanted no more to do with either of them, The Other was in a rage. He beat the wine-server even until he died and removed his right hand and left the woman in the apartment, and the dead man, but took the hand. The Other walked down into the midst of the dancing, and it was night, and many were drunk and had risen to play and they had intercourse and were wild with sin. He took the hand of the wine-server, God have mercy on him, and with much force threw it amongst the revelers and it fell to earth in their midst, but none stopped the revelry, none stopped their sinning, and they danced upon the hand. With that, The Other left me, and I was able to find Abbanes and he, as sickened as I was, agreed to leave this place.

We came to the city of King Hyndopheres[165] and the king asked me if I could build a palace. I knew I could shape stones to make the steps of a palace, but I had never been a master builder, and I knew I could not build an earthly palace for the king. The king's site was unsuitable in any case, with wet earth. I set out instead to build him a palace for his soul by using his resources to sooth the suffering of the poor and sick.

The king sent money for materials, and daily provisions for dozens of men. I took these and went out in the cities and gave to the poor and the afflicted. One day, the king sent messengers, and I responded that the palace was nearly completed and only needed a roof. The king sent gold and silver and, these too, I distributed. I did not praise the king, but gave thanks to God for it, and said to the poor and sick, "It is the Lord God who eases your suffering. He feeds the orphans and widows and heals the sick. Everyone should

---

165 The reader may recognize this king more readily as King Gundafor, but I have left the name as Thomas wrote it in the interest of being true to the document.

learn to end their craving, to not want what they do not have, but a child must eat. With God's help, I will aid your bodily hunger, and then you must quench your spiritual thirst."

As I knew it would, the truth came to the king. I was placed under arrest and brought before the king.

He asked, "Have you built me a palace?"

I said, "I have."

He asked, "When might we see it?"

I said, "You will not see it in this life, but in the next."

He was angered, and had me put into prison. At first, he did not understand the peace that his money and provisions had brought and that they had built for him a better life in the next, but I knew that I would be freed when he embraced the good and felt joy at the suffering he had alleviated.

I remained in prison until the king's brother died and came back to life, with news of the great joy built for the king in the next life, built with the king's money and provisions given to the weak and sick. I was released then and I praised God for showing these men the truth. We went out to the baths, and I baptized them both there, and then the people came to be baptized in the same way and my service to the king ended and my service to God and to Yeshua began anew then.

I built a school[166] there and they learned the scriptures, and the way and teachings of Buddha, and the way and teachings of Yeshua, and we were peaceful and the truth of it was powerful. Many people abandoned false gods and came to us. Our numbers grew, and then I left and moved toward Persia, teaching as I went. As I left each village or city, I put in place a new teacher, a person of the place that understood

---

166 *Closest approximation to the words actually used.*

with clarity and the help of God and could continue the teaching.

Once while I was teaching, a female colt approached. The Other stopped my teaching and was cruel to the ass, and it opened its mouth and began to talk. Many saw the animal, but scarce few heard it speak.

The colt said, "Oh, you who have received the secret counsels of the Nazarene and fellow son of God, you have come amongst lost men so that you might show them how to end their own suffering. Come sit upon me and rest until we reach the next city."

I asked, "Whose colt are you and from where did you come?" I refused, at first, to ride the beast, but he insisted, as did The Other. So, I rode the animal to the gates of the next city and many people followed me. And then I dismounted and told the animal to depart and it fell dead at my feet. The great crowd begged me to bring it back from the dead, but I refused and told them to bury the colt. They did. I could not have raised that which The Other had killed.

41

I spread the words and ideas for many years and to many people and, with The Other, saw more talking beasts and dragons, and I could scarcely keep The Other in check at times. I traveled and so when we fell foul of local rulers, and other people, we were soon gone. Whenever I came back to a village or city, however, I found at least a small group still talking about the way, striving to cease craving and suffering, and speaking of Yeshua.

In all those years, I never told any of them that Yeshua lived north of us, in the mountains, and that he might live there still. I had heard rumors of a teacher from the west, with scars, teaching and baptizing in the ice-cold rivers, that he too was traveling from village to city.

One day, when a man arrived in the village where I was and was inquiring after me, I thought it was another hungry soul. When I met the man, I knew the eyes of Magda in an instant.

"I am Judah ben-Judas, who is called Gebiya.[167] I am the son of Magda and of Judas, called Thomas, the follower of Yeshua of Nazareth. I have traveled for many months from

---

167 "Gebiya" means" goblet." The inference, beyond the boringly obvious, is not apparent.

Vienne[168] in the land of the Keltoi,[169] where my mother birthed me," he said.

"He is more likely the son of Magda and Yeshua," The Other said.

"This is my son," I said.

"You are called Thomas," he said.

I embraced him, and he welcomed me.

"Tell me of your mother," I said.

"I do not care about that woman," The Other said.

Gebiya said, "She lives. She is with my sister."

"Did she marry[170] then?" I asked.

"She found a girl, alone and hungry, and made her into a daughter. She is called Sarah," Gebiya said.

"Does she still live in Vienne?" I asked.

"No, for she murdered a man there, and we fled when I was just a child," Geyiba said.

"Your mother would not kill a man," I said.

"She did."

"Do they hunt her still?" I asked.

"We fled, but in the end, they did not believe he was murdered. They believed he took his own life," Gebiya said.

"But your mother knew him," I said.

"As did you," Geniya said. "He was a Roman of some standing, although he had been exiled to Gaul. He was Pontius Pilatus."

She killed the prefect who crucified Yeshua. The Other laughed.

---

168 Although Vienne was called, "Vienna" by the Romans, it should not be confused with the city now located in Austria. This one is located in modern-day France.

169 Gaul.

170 I simplified here for the sake of clarity.

"Be still," I said.

"Who was it that you told to be still?" Gebiya asked.

I hesitated, but then told him. "There is a voice, he has always been there. I call him the Other."

"Like a shadow you cannot look at directly, but a voice that roars like a storm in your head," Gebiya said.

I was astonished. "You hear one too?"

"All of my life, he has been there," Gebiya said.

I wept! How I wept! I would that my son had been spared this! I cried out to God, asking why my son needed to be so afflicted.

"I kept it a secret, always. My mother taught me to keep the voice a secret, and to not listen to it. It gave me peace to know that you had this also," Gebiya said. "My mother said that she and Yeshua spoke of your second voice at length."

I should have known, for I was sure they discussed all things, late into the nights. I said, "The Other, the voice in my head, has become much more difficult to control, and has even committed evil acts and must be suppressed at every moment. It seems as I grow older and weaker, he becomes more insistent and impulsive."

Gebiya only stared, perhaps considering his own voice. I thought to tell him that the Other had killed man and beast.

"But your mother is well?" I asked.

"She and my sister are well. They teach the words and ideas of Yeshua in their new homeland. The word spreads there, and people listen, even to women," Gebiya said.

"So, you follow the way and the teachings of Yeshua?" I asked.

"I do," he said.

This was good.

"And so, you came to find me?" I asked.

"I did, and I came to ask you to help me," he said.

I waited.

"I want you to help me find Yeshua, and to introduce us," he said.

The journey would be long, and although I too yearned to see Yeshua, I was unsure. I said, "I am no longer a young man."

"Take me to him, that I might finally meet the only husband my mother ever had," Gebiya said.

I thought to dispute this, but I knew this to be true in the truest way. I said, "You might consider that you are the only child birthed by Yeshua's companion and that he might not accept you, except as a symbol of our betrayal of him."

"He will not. He has forgiven you both, else I will not care what he thinks, for if he has not forgiven, he is false!" Gebiya said.

"I will take you, but in way of a bargain, you must return here and we will teach together. As your mother and sister teach in Gaul, we shall teach here as father and son," I said.

"That has been my intention all along," he said. "The two of us."

I thought, in fact, that it would actually be the four of us. The Other agreed.

42

We traveled to Yeshua. When we found him, he was burying his mother. She was placed on a hillside and many people came to see, for the Hindi burned their dead, but Miriam was laid in the custom of her birth-people, in line with the sun's passage.

From that day forward, the people of the region called the place, "The resting place of Mother Miriam."[171]

I shared Yeshua's sadness, but she had been dead for some time and the grief had dulled somewhat for him. We talked for many hours and Gebiya was sad for him as well. Yeshua had grown old as I had, but was more robust than I, although he walked with a bit of difficulty as the injuries from the cross still caused him pain.

About his mother, I asked, "Was she not with Philip? And was he not far west of here?"

Yeshua said, "She lived in a small house in Ephesus, brought there by Philip and Nathanael. Philip stayed and watched over her, and he teaches the people of the region still. When she died they buried her but, after some months,

---

171 This is generally believed to be the modern-day city of Muree, Pakistan. Once known simply as "Mari."

Philip had her taken out and sent to me in a box."[172]

"So Philip still teaches," I said. "But what of Nathanael?" I recalled his laughter and his light manner.

Yeshua's face darkened. "He traveled east and north. There, he taught, but they killed him."

"Was he crucified?" I asked.

"I have been told that he was crucified, or that he was beheaded, but in either account, they removed his skin from his body first, while he still lived," Yeshua said.

This was a true sin. A man of such mirth, with his skin flayed from his body. Then, it was Yeshua who had a question.

He asked, "Gebiya, tell me of your mother."

"She is willful and many listen to her words. Many love her. She speaks of her time here, in this land, as her happiest. She teaches, also, that you were not without flaws. My mother teaches the way and your teachings, but she tells how you sold my father into slavery out of jealousy," Gebiya said.

"I have not been a slave," I said. "I have been on an errand for my brother."

We went to the home of Yeshua and ate. He still had the cup. We drank from it once more. We wondered at how much of the story Gebiya knew. He knew of the cup, of that last meal before Yeshua's arrest, of the crucifixion. He knew of Judas Iscariot, and Simon Kepha, and of the soma and hing. He knew it all. Magda had spared no detail.

We left Yeshua the next day. With a long embrace and kiss, I said goodbye to the man I had known since he was a small child. He embraced my son as well, and looked into his eyes, and I wonder if he was not looking at Magda once more.

---

172 *A box, as in an ossuary.*

"If you ever see your mother again, tell her I love her still," Yeshua said.

"I will never see her again," Gebiya said. "I will minister to the people here."

As we walked away, I looked back time and again, and Yeshua stood there watching us go. Unmoving, arms at his side, and at least until I could no longer see, he smiled a smile of peace.

*   *   *

Once we had returned to the south, Gebiya and I resumed our teaching in earnest. We devised a plan to visit as many villages and cities as possible in the next year, and then in each subsequent year, we returned to each in the same way. From time to time, we heard a bit of news about Yeshua, or from Jerusalem.

Some years later, we were saddened to learn that James the Just had been killed. The priests of Jerusalem had asked James to speak to the people, to calm them, for they loved him and he was the leader of the largest group of people who believed in the message of Yeshua. Then, from the high point near the temple, he fooled the priests and instead called on the people to be steadfast in the teachings and the way. They threw him from that point and he fell, but did not die. Seeing this, they struck him with stones. It was not a good death. It was also distressing because James had been a touchstone[173] that worked against the teachings of Paul of Tarsus, who was insane and did not understand Buddha and the work to end all craving, to be at peace and to not covet anything. He did

---

173 Or perhaps more like an anchor point.

not understand that Yeshua was just a teacher, and was not ever supposed to be a person to be worshipped. True, Yeshua was a son of God, but so were we all sons and daughters of God, and that was so central to what Yeshua taught that to ignore it, to ignore that the true divinity and light was within all of us, was to completely ignore the core of Yeshua's message.

Now, as I write this, I know that my time grows short. I am imprisoned because I baptized and taught and brought light to the son and the wife and the relatives of a certain king Misdaeus, and they knew the truth. His son became a teacher of the way in his own right.

When I first was brought before Misdaeus, he asked me, "Are you servant[174] or free?"

"I am a servant," I said.

"Who is your master?" he asked.

"My master is a master of you and your people, and a master of heaven and earth," I said.

Misdaeus asked, "What is his name?"

I said, "He has had many names and will be known by many more. Most recently, he has a new name, but he has been Yeshua of Nazareth, and before that he was Gyalwa Nagarjuna, and soon he will be someone else."

Misdaeus grew quiet.

"He will kill us," the Other said.

"I know," I said. I looked at my feet. I was tired. "It is time."

"I have not hurried to destroy you. I have been patient with you and your teaching among my people, but your deeds have grown more evil. People speak of your sorcery throughout the land. Now, it has touched my son. I will cleanse the land and your sorcery shall depart with you," he said.

---

174 Bonded.

I told him that I would forgive him, and I do.

*   *   *

I leave all that I am and have to my son, Judah ben-Judas, called Gebiya, chosen by God to spread the word and the light. May those who love me, also truly love him. May those who hate or fear me, be forever blind and deaf and dumb. The Other has been reduced to a shouting madman, clawing inside my skull. He is as condemned as I am. The time grows short. To Magda, I say what you ever knew, that I love you. To Yeshua, I say, thank you. Thank you for being the light and the reason. I will look for you. May you suffer less in the next. Peace be with you all.

Translator's Notes

So ended the writing of Thomas the Apostle. What follows is an apparent addendum, written by his son. This later contribution was actually written in Latin. It was evident that his son had had a formal education. In the interest of continuity, I have attempted to maintain the same sort of diction, syntax, and tone in the translation of the son's writing as I did with the father's. This required quite an effort on my part, since as one might imagine (if one had my set of skills), the translation of Koine Greek versus Latin present significant linguistic differences. I hope the benefits of my efforts are obvious to all.

43

I am called Judah ben-Judas, son of one called Thomas, follower of Yeshua the Nazarene, and of Most Holy Buddha, and of the path. My father was a son of God and a man of peace. Many of the people, including the nobles and those in authority, believed in his teachings. Because of this, King Misdaeus was cautious in his murder of my father.

He took him some distance, with guards, and the people believed that perhaps this was only a dialogue, but some men and I followed close by, since we knew. After we had walked far from the crowd onto a hill, Misdaeus turned Thomas over to an officer with four soldiers. The soldiers carried spears and two walked on his right side and two on his left side. My father was old and the officer helped him and held his arm as they walked, to steady him.

Misdaeus stopped walking but said, "Pierce him with your spears and put an end to this old sorcerer. Then return to the city." King Misdaeus then turned and, with guards, walked back to the city without watching my father's end.

My father saw me and cried out, "Oh, how things are revealed right to the end! I am made of us, my son! And so, I am four! Two of me and two of you! And there are four to cast me down! And I am led by one, as I return to the one who sent me!"

I worried that his madness would be the last words of him.

"Yeshua was just one, and was pierced by one! But my flesh, as you are my flesh as well, contains four and I will be pierced by four!" he said.

When they arrived on the top of the hill, where he was to be slain, he said to all assembled, among which numbered the son of the king, "Do not let the eyes of your heart be blinded, nor your ears be made deaf. Listen to me now, because I come to the time to depart this body. Believe in the God I have taught you, and do not let your hearts harden, for a hard heart is a prison constructed of fear. Walk in freedom and in the light of all men and women. Walk free in the life given you."

My father turned to the king's son, who was a believer and baptized by him, and said, "Convince these servants of Misdaeus to let me pray." And the son of Misdaeus, who himself was called Iuzanes, persuaded the soldiers to let my father pray one last time.

My father went to his knees briefly, silently, and then rose. He spread his arms wide. He prayed, saying, "My Lord and My God, the hope and redeemer and leader in all the lands, be with those who serve you and those who serve their brothers and sisters in your name. Guide me into the next life as I once again seek enlightenment. My soul is yours; please do not let it fall into a life that will not serve you. Let not the serpent who has followed me this whole life follow me one day more, and send the Other from me at last. Behold, Lord, I have done my best to do your work. I was even sold into bond; therefore today I am truly freed. Answer my prayer. I do not doubt you will, but I want all of those who need to hear my prayer, to hear."

All were silent. My father lowered his arms, lowered his head. He said softly to the four soldiers, "Come, with your spears, and fulfill the command of the king who sent you."

From the four corners, with spears they pierced him all at once, and he fell. The soldiers said nothing more and, with the officer, they left. I ran to kneel beside him.

He took my hand. He said, "The Other is already dead. His voice is silenced. I have finally lived without him. Praise be to God."

Then, Judas called Thomas, known also as Didymos, breathed his last.

*   *   *

In the years that followed, I heard of the deaths of many of the others of my father's friends. All in far places. Even Paul of Tarsus was beheaded. The brothers Simon Kepha and Andrew were also crucified, with Andrew's cross on its side and Simon Kepha, it is said, hung upside down. Philip was beheaded as well. Few died a death of nature. One of these was John, the son of Zebedee.

Another was Yeshua. He finally died a very old man. They buried him with his cup, so the test of which my mother once spoke, when a young boy chose it from among many other items, would never be repeated. The cup would never be passed again.

They buried him in his mountains, at the bank of a lake, near a city called Puranadhistan.[175] He was buried in the custom of his original homeland, in line with the sun's

---

175 A city now known as Srinagar. For further discussion of the grave of Yeshua, I refer you to my epilogue at the end of this manuscript.

passage, and his grave marked with the final name he had in this lifetime, which was "Yuzasaf." In the stones, they engraved the likeness of two feet, each foot bearing the mark of a nail. It was understood by all that should the stones ever wear or break, that they were to be replaced so that future people would always know that this truly was the resting place of Yeshua, the teacher from Nazareth.

Epilogue

I am convinced that this accomplishment—this discovery, its rescue, and its translation—represents the zenith of my career, which even humbly I might point out has not been without some well-known successes.

The first-person account as captured by Thomas, the Apostle, is unique and can only have been presented by this particular witness to history. He and I have provided a fresh, and the most accurate, account of the lives of not only Jesus of Nazareth, but also of Mary his mother, Mary Magdalene, and Thomas himself. We have even resolved the mysteries of several miracles, the deaths of Pontius Pilate and of Judas Iscariot; the latter, it appears, has been too harshly judged by history.

We know, directly from one of the conspirators, that Jesus did not die on the cross, but instead survived that terrible ordeal and lived to old age, preaching in northern India.

My work with this manuscript has proven that Yuz-Asaf,[176] was Yeshua, known as Jesus of Nazareth, and that his grave is in a shrine in Srinagar, the capital of Kashmir,

---

176 Also known widely as St. Issa.

in India. I have since traveled to the shrine.

It is a small building known as Roz-Abal, and in need of some maintenance. It is not on the outskirts, but is instead on a street corner within the city.

It is a small stone building, white with muted red trim around its windows, and a green roof. It is not a secret, and appears in India's tourist brochures, including an edition of the Lonely Planet travel guide to India that lists it as a place believed by some to be Jesus's tomb. The locals accept this as fact. They believe that Jesus of Nazareth is buried there, beside a Muslim holy man who was added centuries later.

Inside the stone structure is a smaller wooden chamber. This inner chamber is painted a dark green, with glass-paned windows all around, and ornate trim above these. One can walk completely around the inner chamber, looking in. Inside are boxes, resembling chests, shrouded. However, these do not contain remains. Instead, below these and, indeed, beneath the floor are the remains of two men. One oriented as a Muslim would be, and we can assume these are the remains of the holy man, Mir Sayyid Naserudin. The other oriented as one would bury a Jew.

Above ground, and closest to this older set of remains, is an ancient stone with the shape of footprints crudely carved into it, and polished to a shine. Within these footprints are the clear representations of scars, as would be made during crucifixion.

I do not believe that these facts destroy faith. In fact, all of this taken collectively is an altogether more inspiring story than what we had without the writing of Thomas and his son, Judah. This was not some automaton calmly walking about blurting out maxims, conducting magic tricks, almost without emotion with the exception of a largely unexplained tantrum at the Temple and the weeping and agony leading up to and associated with his death. This was a real human being, struggling to follow the holy scriptures of two belief systems, pulling together what he felt were the best of each in order to start a movement free from suffering and striving for peace.

It is clear that even then, and history certainly bears this out, those who believed in Jesus's work and tried to carry it forward were disturbed by how Paul, formerly known as Saul, was changing the message of Jesus. Unfortunately, due to his evangelizing and the deaths of his competitors such as James the Just, Paul's twisted brand of Jesus's teachings became the foundation for the Church in Rome, which of course has served as the foundation for all Christians since. Even those Christian sects who feel they are completely different from Roman Catholicism, and far removed from the Vatican today, still more closely resemble a church Paul of Tarsus would have founded than one Thomas, James, and even Jesus, would have created.

It is clear from this manuscript, which I am so grateful I was talented enough to bring to light, that the true message of Yeshua was not one of subjugation to God or of perpetual victimhood. Instead, his message was one of realization, that we each have the capacity for happiness, that the root of all of our suffering is wanting what we do not already have, that we each have within ourselves the capability to end our own suffering, and that there is an all-powerful entity in the universe that supports us in these efforts.

I, for one, know I have lived my life that way, and I am grateful to learn that it is what Jesus of Nazareth had promoted more than twenty centuries before. I am deeply honored that I am able now to join the relatively small band of people, mostly men, who have been part of the effort to bring the true message of Jesus to the masses, and that I can perhaps undo some of the damage caused by organized religion over the centuries. From Paul to the Crusades to the Inquisition to modern radical churches spewing hate while claiming to act in Jesus's name, perhaps in my own way I can help to put some of that behind us.

So, in the end, I might consider myself not only to be a scholar, a gentlemen, and a bit of an adventurer, but also perhaps I am the last apostle of Yeshua, still true to the message. By passing along Yeshua's actual intent, with Thomas's help despite his obvious mental illness, perhaps I contribute in a new way to history. I might remove a carefully constructed veil and unleash upon the earth the truth. Who knows where this project of mine may lead? Perhaps a reinvention of religion, or law, or society. Maybe this manuscript, like so many before it, will spur on a new belief system. One never knows. In a century hence, people may look back and point to this writing, and of course my translation of it, as the founding of a new religion, and then people might argue and discuss who the founder truly was. That would be a title I of course would shrug off, but the thought is interesting.

Once more,
—B. L. Treah, Ph.D., Professor of Classics,
University of Cincinnati

Acknowledgments

Nylah Lyman, who was the biggest supporter of this book, throughout the many years of research and writing.

Jason Cote, a good friend of huge talents, who helped with crucial aspects of tone and the nature of translations of ancient documents.

Marta Nesbitt, a terrific and patient editor, and in multiple languages yet. I am grateful for her many hours of work, and brilliant suggestions.

Jamie and Cindy Carpenter, who fed and housed me while the last chapters were written.

Sources found useful while writing this novel included:

Biblegateway.com, newadvent.org, dharmaweb.org, and combinedgospel.com

Young's Literal Translation by Robert Young

New American Standard Bible

The Gospel of Thomas, *The Acts of Thomas*, *The Gospel of Judas*, *The Gospel of Mary*, *The Gospel of Philip*, *The Acts of Peter*

 Pistis Sophia

 The Unknown Life of Jesus Christ by Nicolas Notovitch

A number of BBC documentaries

If interested, one might view video of the tomb in Kashmir at:

http://www.youtube.com/watch?v=7aauXxuLHnQ

About the Author

Kevin St. Jarre is the author of *Aliens, Drywall, and a Unicycle* and *Celestine*, both novels published by Encircle Publications. He previously penned three original thriller novels for Berkley Books, the Night Stalkers series, under a pseudonym. He's a published poet, his pedagogical essays have run in *English Journal* and thrice in *Phi Delta Kappan*, and his short fiction has appeared in journals such as *Story*.

Kevin has worked as a teacher and professor, a newspaper reporter, an international corporate consultant, and he led a combat intelligence team in the first Gulf War. Kevin is a polyglot, and he earned an MFA in Creative Writing with a concentration in Popular Fiction from University of Southern Maine's Stonecoast program. Twice awarded scholarships, he studied at the Norman Mailer Writers Center on Cape Cod, MA, with Sigrid Nunez and David

Black, and wrote in southern France at La Muse Artists & Writers Retreat.

He is a member of the Maine Writers and Publishers Alliance and the International Thriller Writers. Born in Pittsfield, Massachusetts, Kevin grew up in Maine's northernmost town, Madawaska. He now lives on the Maine coast, and is always working on the next novel. Follow Kevin at www.facebook.com/kstjarre and on Twitter @kstjarre.

If you enjoyed reading this book,
please consider writing your honest review
and sharing it with other readers.

Many of our Authors are happy to participate in
Book Club and Reader Group discussions.
For more information, contact us at info@encirclepub.com.

Thank you,
Encircle Publications

For news about more exciting new fiction, join us at:
Facebook: www.facebook.com/encirclepub

Twitter: twitter.com/encirclepub

Instagram: www.instagram.com/encirclepublications

Sign up for Encircle Publications newsletter and specials:
eepurl.com/cs8taP